Conte̶

Sir Noel's Heir

A Novel

May Agnes Fleming

Alpha Editions

This edition published in 2023

ISBN : 9789357953993

Design and Setting By
Alpha Editions
www.alphaedis.com
Email - info@alphaedis.com

CHAPTER I.

SIR NOEL'S DEATH-BED.

The December night had closed in wet and wild around Thetford Towers. It stood down in the low ground, smothered in trees, a tall, gaunt, hoary pile of gray stone, all peaks, and gables and stacks of chimneys, and rook-infested turrets. A queer, massive, old house, built in the days of James the First, by Sir Hugo Thetford, the first baronet of the name, and as staunch and strong now as then.

The December day had been overcast and gloomy, but the December night was stormy and wild. The wind worried and wailed through the tossing trees with whistling moans and shrieks that were desolately human, and made me think of the sobbing banshee of Irish legends. Far away the mighty voice of the stormy sea mingled its hoarse-bass, and the rain lashed the windows in long, slanting lines. A desolate night and a desolate scene without; more desolate still within, for on his bed, this tempestuous winter night, the last of the Thetford baronets lay dying.

Through the driving wind and lashing rain a groom galloped along the high road to the village at break-neck speed. His errand was to Dr. Gale, the village surgeon, which gentleman he found just preparing to go to bed.

"For God's sake, doctor!" cried the man, white as a sheet, "come with me at once! Sir Noel's killed!"

Dr. Gale, albeit phlegmatic, staggered back, and stared at the speaker aghast.

"What? Sir Noel killed?"

"We're afraid so, doctor; none of us knows for certain sure, but he lies there like a dead man. Come quick, for the love of goodness, if you want to do any service!"

"I'll be with you in five minutes," said the doctor, leaving the room to order his horse and don his hat and great coat.

Dr. Gale was as good as his word. In less than ten minutes he and the groom were flying recklessly along to Thetford Tower.

"How did it happen?" asked the doctor, hardly able to speak for the furious pace at which they were going. "I thought he was at Lady Stokestone's ball."

"He did go," replied the groom; "leastways he took my lady there; but he said he had a friend to meet from London at the Royal George to-night, and he rode back. We don't, none of us, know how it happened; for a better or surer rider than Sir Noel there ain't in Devonshire; but Diana must have slipped and threw him. She came galloping in by herself about half an hour ago all blown; and me and three more set off to look for Sir Noel. We found him about twenty yards from the gates, lying on his face in the mud, and as stiff and cold as if he was dead."

"And you brought him home and came for me?"

"Directly, sir. Some wanted to send word to my lady; but Mrs. Hilliard, she thought how you had best see him first, sir, so's we'd know what danger he was really in before alarming her ladyship."

"Quite right, William. Let us trust it may not be serious. Had Sir Noel been—I mean, I suppose he had been dining?"

"Well, doctor," said William, "Arneaud, that's his *valet de chambre*, you know, said he thought he had taken more wine than was prudent going to Lady Stokestone's ball, which her ladyship is very particular about such, you know, sir."

"Ah! that accounts," said the doctor, thoughtfully; "and now William, my man, don't let's talk any more, for I feel completely blown already."

Ten minutes' sharp riding brought them to the great entrance gates of Thetford Towers. An old woman came out of a little lodge, built in the huge masonry, to admit them, and they dashed up the long winding avenue under the surging oaks and chestnuts. Five minutes more and Dr. Gale was running up a polished staircase of black, slippery oak, down an equally wide and black and slippery passage, and into the chamber where Sir Noel lay.

A grand and stately chamber, lofty, dark and wainscoted, where the wax candles made luminous clouds in the darkness, and the wood-fire on the marble hearth failed to give heat. The oak floor was overlaid with Persian rugs; the windows were draped in green velvet and the chairs were upholstered in the same. Near the center of the apartment stood the bed, tall, broad, quaintly carved, curtained in green velvet, and on it, cold and lifeless, lay the wounded man. Mrs. Hilliard, the housekeeper, sat beside him, and Arneaud, the Swiss valet, with a frightened face, stood near the fire.

"Very shocking business this, Mrs. Hilliard," said the doctor, removing his hat and gloves—"very shocking. How is he? Any signs of consciousness yet?"

"None whatever, sir," replied the housekeeper, rising. "I am so thankful you have come. We, none of us, know what to do for him, and it is dreadful to see him lying there like that."

She moved away, leaving the doctor to his examination. Ten minutes, fifteen, twenty passed, then Dr. Gale turned to her with a very pale, grave face.

"It is too late, Mrs. Hilliard. Sir Noel is a dead man!"

"Dead?" repeated Mrs. Hilliard, trembling and holding by a chair. "Oh, my lady! my lady!"

"I am going to bleed him," said the doctor, "to restore consciousness. He may last until morning. Send for Lady Thetford at once."

Arneaud started up. Mrs. Hilliard looked at him, wringing her hands.

"Break it gently, Arneaud. Oh, my lady! my dear lady! So young and so pretty—and only married five months!"

The Swiss valet left the room. Dr. Gale got out his lancet, and desired Mrs. Hilliard to hold the basin. At first the blood refused to flow—but presently it came in a little, feeble stream. The closed eyelids fluttered; there was a restless movement and Sir Noel Thetford opened his eyes in this mortal life once more. He looked first at the doctor, grave and pale, then at the housekeeper, sobbing on her knees by the bed. He was a young man of seven-and-twenty, fair and handsome, as it was in the nature of the Thetfords to be.

"What is it?" he faintly asked. "What is the matter?"

"You are hurt, Sir Noel," the doctor answered, sadly; "you have been thrown from your horse. Don't attempt to move—you are not able."

"I remember—I remember," said the young man, a gleam of recollection lighting up his ghastly face. "Diana slipped, and I was thrown. How long ago is that?"

"About an hour."

"And I am hurt? Badly."

He fixed his eyes with a powerful lock on the doctor's face, and that good man shrunk away from the news he must tell.

"Badly?" reiterated the young baronet, in a peremptory tone, that told all of his nature. "Ah! you won't speak, I see! I am, and I feel—I feel. Doctor, am I going to die?"

He asked the question with a sudden wildness—a sudden horror of death, half starting up in bed. Still the doctor did not speak; still Mrs. Hilliard's suppressed sobs echoed in the stillness of the vast room.

Sir Noel Thetford fell back on his pillow, a shadow as ghastly and awful as death itself lying on his face. But he was a brave man and the descendant of a fearless race; and except for one convulsive throe that shook him from head to foot, nothing told his horror of his sudden fate. There was a weird pause. Sir Noel lay staring straight at the oaken wall, his bloodless face awful in its intensity of hidden feeling. Rain and wind outside rose higher and higher, and beat clamorously at the windows; and still above them, mighty and terrible, rose the far-off voice of the ceaseless sea.

The doctor was the first to speak, in hushed and awe-struck tones.

"My dear Sir Noel, the time is short, and I can do little or nothing. Shall I send for the Rev. Mr. Knight?"

The dying eyes turned upon him with a steady gaze.

"How long have I to live? I want the truth."

"Sir Noel, it is very hard, yet it must be Heaven's will. But a few hours, I fear."

"So soon?" said the dying man. "I did not think——Send for Lady Thetford," he cried, wildly, half raising himself again—"send for Lady Thetford at once!"

"We have sent for her," said the doctor; "she will be here very soon. But the clergyman, Sir Noel—the clergyman. Shall we not send for him?"

"No!" said Sir Noel, sharply. "What do I want of a clergyman? Leave me, both of you. Stay, you can give me something, Gale, to keep up my strength to the last? I shall need it. Now go. I want to see no one but Lady Thetford."

"My lady has come!" cried Mrs. Hilliard, starting to her feet; and at the same moment the door was opened by Arneaud, and a lady in a sparkling ball-dress swept in. She stood for a moment on the threshold, looking from face to face with a bewildered air.

She was very young—scarcely twenty, and unmistakably beautiful. Taller than common, willowy and slight, with great, dark eyes, flowing dark curls, and a colorless olive skin. The darkly handsome face, with pride in every feature, was blanched now almost to the hue of the dying man's; but that glittering, bride-like figure, with its misty point-lace and blazing diamonds, seemed in strange contradiction to the idea of death.

- 4 -

"My lady! my lady!" cried Mrs. Hilliard, with a suppressed sob, moving near her.

The deep, dark eyes turned upon her for an instant, then wandered back to the bed; but she never moved.

"Ada," said Sir Noel, faintly, "come here. The rest of you go. I want no one but my wife."

The graceful figure in its shining robes and jewels, flitted over and dropped on its knees by his side. The other three quitted the room and closed the door. Husband and wife were alone with only death to overhear.

"Ada, my poor girl, only five months a wife—it is very hard on you; but it seems I must go. I have a great deal to say to you, Ada—that I can't die without saying. I have been a villain, Ada—the greatest villain on earth to you."

She had not spoken. She did not speak. She knelt beside him, white and still, looking and listening with strange calm. There was a sort of white horror in her face, but very little of the despairing grief one would naturally look for in the dying man's wife.

"I don't ask you to forgive me, Ada—I have wronged you too deeply for that; but I loved you so dearly—so dearly! Oh, my God! what a lost and cruel wretch I have been."

He lay panting and gasping for breath. There was a draught which Dr. Gale had left standing near, and he made a motion for it. She held it to his lips, and he drank; her hand was unsteady and spilled it, but still she never spoke.

"I cannot speak loudly, Ada," he said, in a husky whisper, "my strength seems to grow less every moment; but I want you to promise me before I begin my story that you will do what I ask. Promise! promise!"

He grasped her wrist and glared at her almost fiercely.

"Promise!" he reiterated. "Promise! promise!"

"I promise," she said, with white lips.

"May Heaven deal with you, Ada Thetford, as you keep that promise. Listen now."

The wild night wore on. The cries of the wind in the trees grew louder and wilder and more desolate. The rain beat and beat against the curtained glass; the candles grettered and flared; and the wood-fire flickered and died out.

And still, long after the midnight hour had tolled, Ada, Lady Thetford, in her lace and silk and jewels, knelt beside her young husband, and listened to the dark and shameful story he had to tell. She never once faltered, she never spoke or stirred; but her face was whiter than her dress, and her great dark eyes dilated with a horror too intense for words.

The voice of the dying man sank lower and lower—it fell to a dull, choking whisper at last.

"You have heard all," he said huskily.

"All?"

The word dropped from her lips like ice—the frozen look of blank horror never left her face.

"And you will keep your promise?"

"Yes."

"God bless you! I can die now! Oh, Ada! I cannot ask you to forgive me; but I love you so much—so much! Kiss me once, Ada, before I go."

His voice failed even with the words. Lady Thetford bent down and kissed him, but her lips were as cold and white as his own.

They were the last words Sir Noel Thetford ever spoke. The restless sea was sullenly ebbing, and the soul of the man was floating away with it. The gray, chill light of a new day was dawning over the Devonshire fields, rainy and raw, and with its first pale ray the soul of Noel Thetford, baronet, left the earth forever.

An hour later, Mrs. Hilliard and Dr. Gale ventured to enter. They had rapped again and again; but there had been no response, and alarmed they had come in. Stark and rigid already lay what was mortal of the Lord of Thetford Towers; and still on her knees, with that frozen look on her face, knelt his living wife.

"My lady! my lady!" cried Mrs. Hilliard, her tears falling like rain. "Oh! my dear lady, come away!"

She looked up; then again at the marble form on the bed, and without a word or cry, slipped back in the old housekeeper's arms in a dead faint.

CHAPTER II.

CAPT. EVERARD.

It was a very grand and stately ceremonial, that funeral procession from Thetford Towers. A week after that stormy December night they laid Sir Noel Thetford in the family vault, where generation after generation of his race slept their last long sleep. The gentry for miles and miles around were there, and among them came the heir-at-law, the Rev. Horace Thetford, only an obscure country curate now, but failing male heirs to Sir Noel, successor to the Thetford estate and fifteen thousand a year.

In a bedchamber, luxurious as wealth can make a room, lay Lady Thetford, dangerously ill. It was not a brain fever exactly, but something very like it into which she had fallen, coming out of the death-like swoon. It was all very sad and shocking—the sudden death of the gay and handsome young baronet, and the serious illness of his poor wife. The funeral oration of the Rev. Mr. Knight, rector of St. Gosport, from the text, "In the midst of life we are in death," was most eloquent and impressive, and women with tender hearts shed tears, and men listened with grave, sad faces. It was such a little while—only five short months—since the wedding-bells had rung, and there had been bonfires and feasting throughout the village; and Sir Noel, looking so proud and so happy, had driven up to the illuminated hall with his handsome bride. Only five months; and now—and now.

The funeral was over and everybody had gone back home—everybody but the Rev. Horace Thetford, who lingered to see the result of my lady's illness, and if she died, to take possession of his estate. It was unutterably dismal in the dark, hushed old house, with Sir Noel's ghost seeming to haunt every room—very dismal and ghastly this waiting to step into dead people's shoes. But then there was fifteen thousand a year, and the finest place in Devonshire; and the Rev. Horace would have faced a whole regiment of ghosts and lived in a vault for that.

But Lady Thetford did not die. Slowly but surely, the fever that had worn her to a shadow left her; and by-and-bye, when the early primroses peeped through the first blackened earth, she was able to come down-stairs—to come down feeble and frail and weak, colorless as death and as silent and cold.

The Rev. Horace went back to Yorkshire, yet not entirely in despair. Female heirs could not inherit Thetford—he stood a chance yet; and the widow, not yet twenty, was left alone in the dreary old mansion. People were very sorry for her, and came to see her, and begged her to be resigned to her great loss; and Mr. Knight preached endless homilies on patience, and hope, and submission, and Lady Thetford listened to them just as if they had been talking Greek. She never spoke of her dead husband—she shivered at the mention of his name; but that night at his dying bed had changed her as never woman changed before. From a bright, ambitious, pleasure-loving girl, she had grown into a silent, haggard, hopeless woman. All the sunny spring days she sat by the window of her boudoir, gazing at the misty, boundless sea, pale and mute—dead in life.

The friends who came to see her, and Mr. Knight, the rector, were a little puzzled by this abnormal case, but very sorry for the pale young widow, and disposed to think better of her than ever before. It must surely have been the vilest slander that she had not cared for her husband, that she had married him only for his wealth and title; and that young soldier—that captain of dragoons—must have been a myth. She might have been engaged to him, of course, before Sir Noel came, that seemed to be an undisputed fact; and she might have jilted him for a wealthier lover, that was all a common case. But she must have loved her husband very dearly, or she never would have been broken-hearted like this at his loss.

Spring deepened into summer. The June roses in the flower-gardens of the Thetford were in rosy bloom, and my lady was ill again—very, very ill. There was an eminent physician down from London, and there was a frail little mite of babyhood lying among lace and flannel; and the eminent physician shook his head, and looked portentously grave as he glanced from the crib to the bed. Whiter than the pillows, whiter than snow, Ada, Lady Thetford, lay, hovering in the Valley of the Shadow of Death; that other feeble little life seemed flickering, too—it was so even a toss up between the great rival powers, Life and Death, that a straw might have turned the scale either way. So slight being that baby-hold of gasping breath, that Mr. Knight, in the absence of any higher authority, and in the unconsciousness of the mother, took it upon himself to baptize it. So a china bowl was brought, and Mrs. Hilliard held the bundle of flannel and long white robes, and the child was named—the name which the mother had said weeks ago it was to be called, if a boy—Rupert Noel Vandeleur Thetford; for it was a male heir, and the Rev. Horace's cake was dough.

Days went by, weeks, months, and to the surprise of the eminent physician neither mother nor child died. Summer waned, winter returned; and the anniversary of Sir Noel's death came round, and my lady was able to walk down-stairs, shivering in the warm air under all her wraps. She had expressed no pleasure or thankfulness in her own safety, or that of her child. She had asked eagerly if it were a boy or a girl; and hearing its sex, had turned her face to the wall, and lay for hours and hours speechless and motionless. Yet it was very dear to her, too, by fits and starts as it were. She would hold it in her arms half a day, sometimes covering it with kisses, with jealous, passionate love, crying over it, and half smothering it with caresses; and then, again, in a fit of sullen apathy, would resign it to its nurse, and not ask to see it for hours. It was very strange and inexplicable, her conduct, altogether; more especially, as with her return to health came no return of cheerfulness and hope. The dark gloom that overshadowed her life seemed to settle into a chronic disease, rooted and incurable. She never went out; she returned no visits; she gave no invitations to those who came to repeat theirs. Gradually people fell off; they grew tired of that sullen coldness in which Lady Thetford wrapped herself as in a mantle, until Mr. Knight and Dr. Gale grew to be almost her only visitors. "Mariana, in the Moated Grange," never led a more solitary and dreary existence than the handsome young widow, who dwelt a recluse at Thetford Towers; for she was very handsome still, of a pale moonlit sort of beauty, the great, dark eyes, and abundant dark hair, making her fixed and changeless pallor all the more remarkable.

Months and seasons went by. Summers followed winters, and Lady Thetford still buried herself alive in the gray old manor—and the little heir was six years old. A delicate child still, puny and sickly, and petted and spoiled, and indulged in every childish whim and caprice. His mother's image and idol—no look of the fair-haired, sanguine, blue-eyed Thetford sturdiness in his little, pinched, pale face, large, dark eyes, and crisp, black ringlets. The years had gone by like a slow dream; life was stagnant enough in St. Gosport, doubly stagnant at Thetford Towers, whose mistress rarely went abroad beyond her own gates, save when she took her little son out for an airing in the pony phaeton.

She had taken him out for one of those airings on a July afternoon, when he had nearly accomplished his seventh year. They had driven seaward some miles from the manor-house, and Lady Thetford and her little boy had got out, and were strolling leisurely up and down the hot, white stands, while the groom waited with the pony-phaeton just within sight.

The long July afternoon wore on. The sun that had blazed all day like a wheel of fire, dropped lower and lower into the crimson west. The wide sea shone red with the reflections of the lurid glory in the heavens, and the numberless waves glittered and flashed as if sown with stars. A faint, far-off breeze swept over the sea, salt and cold; and the fishermen's boats danced along with the red sunset glinting on their sails.

Up and down, slowly and thoughtfully, the lady walked, her eyes fixed on the wide sea. As the rising breeze met her, she drew the scarlet shawl she wore over her black silk dress closer around her, and glanced at her boy.

The little fellow was running over the sands, tossing pebbles into the surf, and hunting for shells; and her eyes left him and wandered once more to the lurid splendor of that sunset on the sea. It was very quiet here, with no living thing in sight but themselves; so the lady's start of astonishment was natural when, turning an abrupt angle in the path leading to the shore, she saw a man coming toward her over the sands. A tall, powerful-looking man of thirty, bronzed and handsome, and with an unmistakably military air, although in plain black clothes. The lady took a second look, then stood stock still, and gazed like one in a dream. The man approached, lifted his hat, and stood silent and grave before her.

"Captain Everard!"

"Yes, Lady Thetford—after eight years—Captain Everard again."

The deep, strong voice suited the bronzed, grave face, and both had a peculiar power of their own. Lady Thetford, very, very pale, held out one fair jeweled hand.

"Captain Everard, I am very glad to see you again."

He bent over the little hand a moment, then dropped it, and stood looking at her silent.

"I thought you were in India," she said, trying to be at ease. "When did you return?"

"A month ago. My wife is dead. I, too, am widowed, Lady Thetford."

"I am very sorry to hear it," she said, gravely. "Did she die in India?"

"Yes; and I have come home with my little daughter."

"Your daughter! Then she left a child?"

"One. It is on her account I have come. The climate killed her mother. I had mercy on her daughter, and have brought her home."

"I am sorry for your wife. Why did she remain in India?"

"Because she preferred death to leaving me. She loved me, Lady Thetford!"

His powerful eyes were on her face—that pale, beautiful face, into which the blood came for an instant at his words. She looked at him, then away over the darkening sea.

"And you, my lady—you gained the desire to your heart, wealth, and a title? Let me hope they have made you a happy woman."

"I am not happy!"

"No? But you have been—you were while Sir Noel lived?"

"My husband was very good to me, Captain Everard. His death was the greatest misfortune that could have befallen me."

"But you are young, you are free, you are rich, you are beautiful. You may wear a coronet next time."

His face and glance were so darkly grave, that the covert sneer was almost hidden. But she felt it.

"I shall never marry again, Captain Everard."

"Never? You surprise me! Six years—nay, seven, a widow, and with innumerable attractions. Oh, you cannot mean it!"

She made a sudden, passionate gesture—looked at him, then away.

"It is useless—worse than useless, folly, madness, to lift the veil from the irrevocable past. But don't you think, don't you, Lady Thetford, that you might have been equally happy if you had married *me*?"

She made no reply. She stood gazing seaward, cold and still.

"I was madly, insanely, absurdly in love with pretty Ada Vandeleur in those days, and I think I would have made her a good husband; better, however—forgive me—than I ever made my poor dead wife. But you were wise and ambitious, my pretty Ada, and bartered your black eyes and raven ringlets to a higher bidder. You jilted me in cold blood, poor love-sick devil that I was, and reigned resplendent as my Lady Thetford. Ah! you knew how to choose the better part, my pretty Ada!"

"Captain Everard, I am sorry for the past—I have atoned, if suffering can atone. Have a little pity, and let me alone!"

He stood and looked at her silently, gravely. Then said, in a voice deep and calm:

"We are both free! Will you marry me now, Ada!"

"I cannot!"

"But I love you—I have always loved you. And you—I used to think you loved me!"

He was strangely calm and passionless, voice and glance and face. But Lady Thetford had covered *her* face, and was sobbing.

"I did—I do—I always have! But I cannot marry you. I will love you all my life; but don't, *don't* ask me to be your wife!"

"As you please!" he said, in the same passionless voice. "I think it is best myself; for the George Everard of to-day is not the George Everard who loved you eight years ago. We would not be happy—I know that. Ada, is that your son?"

"Yes."

"I should like to look at him. Here, my little baronet! I want to see you."

The boy, who had been looking curiously at the stranger, ran up at a sign from his mother. The tall captain lifted him in his arms and gazed in his small, thin face, with which his bright tartan plaid contrasted harshly.

"He hasn't a look of the Thetfords. He is your own son, Ada. My little baronet, what is your name?"

"Sir Rupert Thetford," answered the child, struggling to get free. "Let me go—I don't know you!"

The captain set him down with a grim smile; and the boy clung to his mother's skirts, and eyed the tall stranger askance.

"I want to go home, mamma! I'm tired and hungry."

"Presently, dearest. Run to William, he has cake for you. Captain Everard, I shall be happy to have you at dinner."

"Thanks; but I must decline. I go back to London to-night. I sail for India again in a week."

"So soon! I thought you meant to remain."

"Nothing is further from my intentions. I merely brought my little girl over to provide her a home; that is why I have troubled *you*. Will you do me this kindness, Lady Thetford?"

"Take your little girl? Oh, most gladly—most willingly!"

"Thanks! Her mother's people are French, and I know little about them; and, save yourself, I can claim friendship with few in England. She will be poor; I have settled on her all I am worth—some three hundred a year; and you, Lady Thetford, you can teach her, when she grows up, to catch a rich husband."

She took no notice of the taunt; she looked only too happy to render him this service.

"I am so pleased! She will be such a nice companion for Rupert. How old is she?"

"Nearly four."

"Is she here?"

"No; she is in London. I will fetch her down in a day or two."

"What do you call her?"

"Mabel—after her mother. Then it is settled, Lady Thetford, I am to fetch her?"

"I shall be delighted! But won't you dine with me?"

"No. I must catch the evening train. Farewell, Lady Thetford, and many thanks! In three days I will be here again."

He lifted his hat and walked away. Lady Thetford watched him out of sight, and then turned slowly, as she heard her little boy calling her with shrill impatience. The red sunset had faded out; the sea lay gray and cold under the twilight sky, and the evening breeze was chill. Changes in sky and sea and land told of coming night; and Lady Thetford, shivering slightly in the rising wind, hurried away to be driven home.

CHAPTER III.

"LITTLE MAY."

On the evening of the third day after this interview, a fly from the railway drove up the long, winding avenue leading to the great front entrance of the Thetford mansion. A bronzed military gentleman, a nurse and a little girl, occupied the fly, and the gentleman's keen, dark eyes wandered searchingly around. Swelling meadows, velvety lawns, sloping terraces, waving trees, bright flower-gardens, quaint old fish-ponds, sparkling fountains, and a wooded park, with sprightly deer—that was what he saw, all bathed in the golden halo of the summer sunset. Massive and grand, the old house reared its gray head, half overgrown with ivy and climbing roses. Gaudy peacocks strutted on the terraces; a graceful gazelle flitted out for an instant amongst the trees to look at them and then fled in afright; and the barking of half a dozen mastiffs greeted their approach noisily.

"A fine old place," thought Captain Everard. "My pretty Ada might have done worse. A grand old place for that puny child to inherit. The staunch old warrior-blood of the Thetfords is sadly adulterated in his pale veins, I fancy. Well, my little May, and how are you going to like all this?"

The child, a bright-faced little creature, with great sparkling eyes and rose-bloom cheeks, was looking in delight at a distant terrace.

"See, papa! See all the pretty peacocks! Look, Ellen," to the nurse, "three, four, five! Oh, how pretty!"

"Then little May will like to live here, where she can see the pretty peacocks every day?"

"And all the pretty flowers, and the water, and the little boy—where's the little boy, papa?"

"In the house—you'll see him presently; but you must be very good, little May, and not pull his hair, and scratch his face, and poke your fingers in his eyes, like you used to do with Willie Brandon. Little May must learn to be good."

Little May put one rosy finger in her mouth, and set her head on one side like a defiant canary. She was one of the prettiest little fairies imaginable, with her pale, flaxen curls, and sparkling light-gray eyes, and apple-blossom complexion; but she was evidently as much spoiled as little Sir Rupert Thetford himself.

Lady Thetford sat in the long drawing-room, after her solitary dinner, and little Sir Rupert played with his rocking-horse and a pile of picture-books in a remote corner. The young widow lay back in the violet-velvet depths of a carved and gilded *fauteuil*, very simply dressed in black and crimson, but looking very fair and stately withal. She was watching her boy with a half smile on her face, when a footman entered with Captain Everard's card. Lady Thetford looked up eagerly.

"Show Captain Everard up at once."

The footman bowed and disappeared. Five minutes later, and the tall captain and his little daughter stood before her.

"At last!" said Lady Thetford, rising and holding out her hand to her old lover, with a smile that reminded him of other days—"at last, when I was growing tired waiting. And this is your little girl—my little girl from henceforth? Come here, my pet, and kiss your new mamma."

She bent over the little one, kissing the pink cheeks and rosy lips.

"She is fair and tiny—a very fairy; but she resembles you, nevertheless, Capt. Everard."

"In temper—yes," said the captain. "You will find her spoiled, and willful, and cross, and capricious and no end of trouble. Won't she, May?"

"She will be the better match for Rupert on that account," Lady Thetford said, smiling, and unfastening little Miss Everard's wraps with her own fair fingers. "Come here, Rupert, and welcome your new sister."

The young baronet approached, and dutifully kissed little May, who put up her rose-bud mouth right willingly. Sir Rupert Thetford wasn't tall, rather undersized, and delicate for his seven years; but he was head and shoulders over the flaxen-haired fairy, with the bright gray eyes.

"I want a ride on your rocking-horse," cried little May, fraternizing with him at once; "and oh! what nice picture books and what a lot!"

The children ran off together to their distant corner, and Captain Everard sat down for the first time.

"You have not dined?" said Lady Thetford. "Allow me to——" her hand was on the bell, but the captain interposed.

"Many thanks—nothing. We dined at the village; and I leave again by the seven-fifty train. It is past seven now, so I have but little time to spare. I fear I am putting you to a great deal of trouble; but May's nurse insists on being taken back to London to-night."

"It will be of no consequence," replied Lady Thetford, "Rupert's nurse will take charge of her. I intend to advertise for a nursery governess in a few days. Rupert's health has always been so extremely delicate, that he has not even began a pretext of learning yet, and it is quite time. He grows stronger, I fancy; but Dr. Gale tells me frankly his constitution is dangerously weak."

She sighed as she spoke, and looked over to where he stood beside little May, who had mounted the rocking-horse boy-fashion. Sir Rupert was expostulating.

"You oughtn't to sit that way—ask mamma. You ought to sit side-saddle. Only boys sit like that."

"I don't care!" retorted Miss Everard, rocking more violently than ever. "I'll sit whatever way I like! Let me alone!"

Lady Thetford looked at the captain with a smile.

"Her father's daughter, surely! bent on having her own way. What a fairy it is! and yet such a perfect picture of health."

"Mabel was never ill an hour in her life, I believe," said her father; "she is not at all too good for this world. I only hope she may not grow up the torment of your life—she is thoroughly spoiled."

"And I fear if she were not, I should do it. Ah! I expect she will be a great comfort to me, and a world of good to Rupert. He has never had a playmate of his own years, and children need children as much as they need sunshine."

They sat for ten minutes conversing gravely, chiefly on business matters connected with little May's annuity—not at all as they had conversed three days before by the seaside. Then, as half-past seven drew near, the captain arose.

"I must go; I will hardly be in time as it is. Come here, little May, and bid papa good-bye."

"Let papa come to May," responded his daughter, still rocking. "I can't get off."

Captain Everard laughed, went over, bent down and kissed her.

"Good-bye, May; don't forget papa, and learn to be a good girl. Good bye, baronet; try and grow strong and tall. Farewell, Lady Thetford, with my best thanks."

She held his hand, looking up in his sun-burned face with tears in her dark eyes.

"We may never meet again, Captain Everard," she said hurriedly. "Tell me before we part that you forgive me the past."

"Truly, Ada, and for the first time. The service you have rendered me fully atones. You should have been my child's mother—be a mother to her now. Good-bye, and God bless you and your boy!"

He stooped over, touched her cheek with his lips reverentially, and then was gone. Gone forever—never to meet those he left behind this side of eternity.

Little May bore the loss of papa and nurse with philosophical indifference—her new playmate sufficed for both. The children took to one another with the readiness of childhood—Rupert all the more readily that he had never before had a playmate of his own years. He was naturally a quiet child, caring more for his picture-books and his nurse's stories than for tops, or balls, or marbles. But little May Everard seemed from the first to inspire him with some of her own superabundant vitality and life. The child was never, for a single instant, quiet; she was the most restless, the most impetuous, the most vigorous little creature that can be conceived. Feet and tongue and hands never were still from morning till night; and the life of Sir Rupert's nurse, hitherto one of idle ease, became all at once a misery to her. The little girl was everywhere—everywhere; especially where she had no business to be; and nurse never knew an easy moment for trotting after her, and rescuing her from all sorts of perils. She could climb like a cat, or a goat, and risked her neck about twenty times per diem; she sailed her shoes in the soup when let in as a treat to dinner, and washed her hands in her milk-and-water. She became the intimate friend of the pretty peacocks and the big, good-tempered dogs, with whom, in utter fearlessness, she rolled about in the grass half the day. She broke young Rupert's toys, and tore his picture-books and slapped his face, and pulled his hair, and made herself master of the situation before she had been twenty-four hours in the house. She was thoroughly and completely spoiled. What India nurses had left undone, injudicious petting and flattery on the homeward passage had completed—and her temper was something appalling. Her shrieks of passion at the slightest contradiction of her imperial will rang through the house, and rent the tortured tympanums of all who heard. The little Xantippe would fling herself flat on the carpet, and literally scream herself black in the face, until, in dread of apoplexy and sudden death, her frightened hearers hastened to yield. Of course, one such victory insured all the rest. As for Sir Rupert, before she had been a week at Thetford Towers, he dared not call his soul his own. She had partly scalped him on several occasions, and left the mark of her cat-like nails in his tender visage: but her venomous power of screeching for hours at will had more to do with the little baronet's dread of her than anything else. He fled ingloriously in every battle—running in tears to mamma, and leaving the field and the trophies of victory triumphantly to Miss Everard. With all this, when not thwarted—when allowed to smash toys, and dirty her clothes, and smear her infantile face, and tear pictures, and torment inoffensive lapdogs; when allowed, in short, to follow "her own sweet will," little May was as charming a fairy as ever the sun shone on. Her gleeful laugh made music in the dreary old rooms, such as had never been heard there for many a day, and her mischievous antics were the delight of all who did not suffer thereby. The servants petted and indulged her, and fed her on unwholesome cakes and sweetmeats, and made her worse and worse every day of her life.

Lady Thetford saw all this with inward apprehension. If her ward was completely beyond her power of control at four, what would she be a dozen years hence?

"Her father was right," thought the lady. "I am afraid she *will* give me a great deal of trouble. I never saw so headstrong, so utterly unmanageable a child."

But Lady Thetford was very fond of the fairy despot withal. When her son came running to her for succor, drowned in tears, his mother took him in her arms and kissed him and soothed him—but she never punished the offender. As for Sir Rupert, he might fly ignominiously, but he never fought back. Little May had all the hair-pulling and face-scratching to herself.

"I must get a governess," mused Lady Thetford. "I may find one who can control this little vixen; and it is really time Rupert began his studies. I shall speak to Mr. Knight about it."

Lady Thetford sent that very day to the rectory her ladyship's compliments, the servant said, and would Mr. Knight call at his earliest convenience. Mr. Knight sent in answer to expect him that same evening; and on his way he fell in with Dr. Gale, going to the manor-house on a professional visit.

"Little Sir Rupert keeps weakly," he said; "no constitution to speak of. Not at all like the Thetfords—splendid old stock, the Thetfords, but run out—run out. Sir Rupert is a Vandeleur, inherits his mother's constitution—delicate child, very."

"Have you seen Lady Thetford's ward!" inquired the clergyman, smiling; "no hereditary weakness there, I fancy. I'll answer for the strength of her lungs, at any rate. The other day she wanted Lady Thetford's watch for a plaything; she couldn't have it, and down she fell flat on the floor in what her nurse calls 'one of her tantrums.' You should have heard her, her shrieks were appalling."

"I have," said the doctor, with emphasis; "she has the temper of the old demon. If I had anything to do with that child, I should whip her within an inch of her life—that's all she wants, lots of whipping! The Lord only knows the future, but I pity her prospective husband!"

"The taming of the shrew," laughed Mr. Knight. "Katherine and Petruchio over again. For my part, I think Lady Thetford was unwise to undertake such a charge. With her delicate health it is altogether too much for her."

The two gentlemen were shown into the library, whilst the servant went to inform his lady of their arrival. The library had a French window opening on a sloping lawn, and here chasing butterflies in high glee, were the two children—the pale, dark-eyed baronet, and the flaxen-tressed little East Indian.

"Look," said Dr. Gale. "Is Sir Rupert going to be your Petruchio? Who knows what the future may bring forth—who knows that we do not behold a future Lady Thetford?"

"She is very pretty," said the rector thoughtfully, "and she may change with years. Your prophecy may be fulfilled."

The present Lady Thetford entered as he spoke. She had heard the remarks of both, and there was an unusual pallor and gravity in her face as she advanced to receive them.

Little Sir Rupert was called in, and May followed, with a butterfly crushed to death in each fat little hand.

"She kills them as fast as she catches them," said Sir Rupert, ruefully. "It's cruel, isn't it, mamma?"

Little May, quite unabashed, displayed her dead prizes, and cut short the doctor's conference by impatiently pulling her play-fellow away.

"Come, Rupert, come," she cried. "I want to catch the black one with the yellow wings. Stick your tongue out and come."

Sir Rupert displayed his tongue, and submitted his pulse to the doctor, and let himself be pulled away by May.

"The gray mare in that span is decidedly the better horse," laughed the doctor. "What a little despot in pinafores it is."

When her visitors had left, Lady Thetford walked to the window and stood watching the two children racing in the sunshine. It was a pretty sight, but the lady's face was contracted with pain.

"No, no," she thought. "I hope not—I pray not. Strange! but I never thought of the possibility before. She will be poor, and Rupert must marry a rich wife, so that if——"

She paused, with a sort of shudder, then added:

"What will he think, my darling boy, of his father and mother if that day ever comes?"

CHAPTER IV.

MRS. WEYMORE.

Lady Thetford had settled her business satisfactorily with the rector of St Gosport.

"Nothing could be more opportune," he said. "I am going to London next week on business which will detain me upward of a fortnight. I will immediately advertise for such a person as you want."

"You must understand," said her ladyship, "I do not require a young girl. I wish a middle-aged person—a widow, for instance, who has had children of her own. Both Rupert and May are spoiled—May particularly is perfectly unmanageable. A young girl as governess for her would never do."

Mr. Knight departed with these instructions and the following week started for the great metropolis. An advertisement was at once inserted in the *Times* newspaper, stating all Lady Thetford's requirements, and desiring immediate application. Another week later, and Lady Thetford received the following communication:

> "DEAR LADY THETFORD—I have been fairly besieged with applications for the past week—all widows, and all professing to be thoroughly competent. Clergyman's widows, doctors' widows, officers' widows—all sorts of widows. I never before thought so many could apply for one situation. I have chosen one in sheer desperation—the widow of a country gentleman in distressed circumstances, who, I think, will suit. She is eminently respectable in appearance, quiet and lady-like in manner, with five years' experience in the nursery-governess line, and the highest recommendation from her late employers. She has lost a child, she tells me, and from her looks and manner altogether, I should judge she was a person conversant with misfortune. She will return with me early next week—her name is Mrs. Weymore."

Lady Thetford read this letter with a little sigh of relief—some one else would have the temper and outbreaks of little May to contend with now. She wrote to Captain Everard that same day, to announce his daughter's well-being, and inform him that she had found a suitable governess to take charge of her.

The second day of the ensuing week the rector and the new governess arrived. A fly from the railway brought her and her luggage to Thetford Towers late in the afternoon, and she was taken at once to the room that had been prepared for her, whilst the servant went to inform Lady Thetford of her arrival.

"Fetch her here at once," said her ladyship, who was alone, as usual, in the long drawing-room with the children, "I wish to see her."

Ten minutes after the drawing-room door was flung open, and "Mrs. Weymore, my lady," announced the footman.

Lady Thetford arose to receive her new dependent, who bowed and stood before her with a somewhat fluttered and embarrassed air. She was quite young, not older than my lady herself, and eminently good-looking. The tall, slender figure, clad in widow's weeds, was as symmetrical as Lady Thetford's own, and the full black dress set off the pearly fairness of the blonde skin, and the rich abundance of fair hair. Lady Thetford's brows contracted a little; her fair, subdued, gentle-looking, girlish young woman, was hardly the strong-minded, middle-aged matron she had expected to take the nonsense out of obstreperous May Everard.

"Mrs. Weymore, I believe," said Lady Thetford, resuming her *fauteuil*, "pray be seated. I wished to see you at once, because I am going out this evening. You have had five years' experience as a nursery-governess, Mr. Knight tells me."

"Yes, my lady."

There was a little tremor in Mrs. Weymore's low voice, and her blue eyes shifted and fell under Lady Thetford's steady and somewhat haughty gaze.

"Yet you look young—much younger than I imagined, or wished."

"I am twenty-seven years old, my lady."

That was my lady's own age precisely, but she looked half a dozen years the elder of the two.

"Are you a native of London?"

"No, my lady, of Berkshire."

"And you have been a widow, how long?"

What ailed Mrs. Weymore? She was all white and trembling—even her hands, folded and pressed together in her lap, shook in spite of her.

"Eight years and more."

She said it with a sort of sob, hysterically choked. Lady Thetford looked on surprised, and a trifle displeased. She was a very proud woman, and certainly wished for no scene with her hired dependents.

"Eight years is a tolerable time," she said, coolly. "You have lost children?"

"One, my lady."

Again that choked, hysterical sob. My lady vent on pitilessly.

"Is it long ago?"

"When—when I lost its father?"

"Ah! both together? That was rather hard. Well, I hope you understand the management of children—spoiled ones particularly. Here are the two you are to take charge of. Rupert—May come here."

The children came over from their corner. Mrs. Weymore drew May toward her, but Sir Rupert held aloof.

"This is my ward—this is my son. I presume Mr. Knight has told you. If you can subdue the temper of that child, you will prove yourself, indeed, a treasure. The east parlor has been fitted up for your use; the children will take their meals there with you; the room adjoining is to be the school-room. I have appointed one of the maids to wait on you. I trust you will find your chamber comfortable."

"Exceedingly so, my lady."

"And the terms proposed by Mr. Knight suit you?"

Mrs. Weymore bowed. Lady Thetford rose to close the interview.

"You must need refreshment and rest after your journey. I will not detain you longer. To-morrow your duties will commence."

She rang the bell—directed the servant who came to show the governess to the east parlor and see to her wants, and then to send nurse for the children. Fifteen minutes after she drove away in the pony-phaeton, whilst the new governess stood by the window of the east parlor and watched her vanish in the amber haze of the August sunset.

Lady Thetford's business in St. Gosport detained her a couple of hours. The big, white, August moon was rising as she drove slowly homeward, and the nightingales sang its vesper lay in the scented hedge-rows. As she passed the rectory she saw Mr. Knight leaning over his own gate enjoying the placid beauty of the summer evening, and Lady Thetford reined in her ponies to speak to him.

"So happy to see your ladyship! Won't you alight and come in? Mrs. Knight will be delighted."

"Not this evening, I think. Had you much trouble about my business?"

"I had applicants enough, certainly," laughed the rector. "I had reason to remember Mr. Weller's immortal advice, 'Beware of widders.' How do you like your governess?"

"I have hardly had time to form an opinion. She is younger than I could desire."

"She looks much younger than the age she gives, I know; but that is a common case. I trust my choice will prove satisfactory—her references are excellent. Your ladyship has had an interview with her?"

"A very brief one. Her manner struck me unpleasantly—so odd, and shy, and nervous. I hardly know how to characterize it; but she may be a paragon of governesses, for all that. Good evening; best regards to Mrs. Knight. Call soon and see how your *protégé* gets on."

Lady Thetford drove away. As she alighted from the pony-carriage and ascended the great front steps of the house, she saw the pale governess still seated at the window of the east parlor, gazing dejectedly out at the silvery moonlight.

"A most woeful countenance," thought my lady. "There is some deeper grief than the loss of a husband and child eight years ago, the matter with that woman. I don't like her."

No, Lady Thetford did not like the meek and submissive looking governess, but the children and the rest of the household did. Sir Rupert and little May took to her at once—her gentle voice, her tender smile seemed to win its way to their capricious favor; and before the end of the first week she had more influence over them than mother and nurse together. The subdued and gentle governess soon had the love of all at Thetford Towers, except its mistress, from Mrs. Hilliard, the stately housekeeper, down. She was courteous and considerate, so anxious to avoid giving trouble. Above all, that fixed expression of hopeless trouble on her sad, pale face, made its way to every heart. She had full charge of the children now; they took their meals with her, and she had them in her keeping the best part of the day—an office that was no sinecure. When they were with their nurse, or my lady, the governess sat alone in the east parlor, looking out dreamily at the summer landscape, with her own brooding thoughts.

One evening when she had been at Thetford Towers over a fortnight, Mrs. Hilliard, coming in, found her sitting dreamily by herself neither reading nor working. The children were in the drawing-room, and her duties were over for the day.

"I am afraid you don't make yourself at home here," said the good-natured housekeeper; "you stay too much alone, and it isn't good for young people like you."

"I am used to solitude," replied the governess with a smile, that ended in a sigh, "and I have grown to like it. Will you take a seat?"

"No," said Mrs. Hilliard. "I heard you say the other day you would like to go over the house; so, as I have a couple of hours leisure, I will show it to you now."

The governess rose eagerly.

"I have been wanting to see it so much," she said, "but I feared to give trouble by asking. It is very good of you to think of me, dear Mrs. Hilliard."

"She isn't much used to people thinking of her," reflected the housekeeper, "or she wouldn't be so grateful for trifles. Let me see," aloud, "you have seen the drawing-room and library, and that is all, except your own apartments. Well, come this way, I'll show you the old south wing."

Through the long corridors, up wide, black, slippery staircases, into vast, unused rooms, where ghostly echoes and darkness had it all to themselves, Mrs. Hilliard led the governess.

"These apartments have been unused since before the late Sir Noel's time," said Mrs. Hilliard; "his father kept them full in the hunting season, and at Christmas time. Since Sir Noel's death, my lady has shut herself up and received no company, and gone nowhere. She is beginning to go out more of late than she has done ever since his death."

Mrs. Hilliard was not looking at the governess, or she might have been surprised at the nervous restlessness and agitation of her manner, as she listened to these very commonplace remarks.

"Lady Thetford was very much attached to her husband, then?" Mrs. Weymore said, her voice tremulous.

"Ah! that she was! She must have been, for his death nearly killed her. It was sudden enough, and shocking enough, goodness knows! I shall never forget that dreadful night. This is the old banqueting-hall, Mrs. Weymore, the largest and dreariest room in the house."

Mrs. Weymore, trembling very much, either with cold or that unaccountable nervousness of hers, hardly looked round at the vast wilderness of a room.

"You were with the late Sir Noel, then, when he died?"

"Yes, until my lady came. Ah! it was a dreadful thing! He had taken her to a ball, and riding home his horse threw him. We sent for the doctor and my lady at once; and when she came, all white and scared like, he sent us out of the room. He was as calm and sensible as you or me, but he seemed to have something on his mind. My lady was shut up with him for about three hours, and then we went in—Dr. Gale and me. I shall never forget that sad sight. Poor Sir Noel was dead, and she was kneeling beside him in her ball dress, like somebody turned to stone. I spoke to her, and she looked up at me, and then fell back in my arms in a fainting fit. Are you cold, Mrs. Weymore, that you shake so?"

"No—yes—it is this desolate room, I think," the governess answered, hardly able to speak.

"It *is* desolate. Come, I'll show you the billiard-room, and then we'll go up-stairs to the room Sir Noel died in. Everything remains just as it was—no one has ever slept there since. If you only knew, Mrs. Weymore, what a sad time it was; but you do know, poor dear! you have lost a husband yourself!"

The governess flung up her hands before her face with a suppressed cry so full of anguish that the housekeeper stared at her aghast. Almost as quickly she recovered herself again.

"Don't mind me," she said, in a choking voice, "I can't help it. You don't know what I suffered—what I still suffer. Oh, pray, don't mind me!"

"Certainly not my dear," said Mrs. Hilliard, thinking inwardly the governess was a very odd person, indeed.

They looked at the billiard-room, where the tables stood, dusty and disused, and the balls lay idly by.

"I don't know when it will be used again," said Mrs. Hilliard; "perhaps not until Sir Rupert grows up. There was a time," lowering her voice, "that I thought he would never live to be as old and strong as he is now. He was the puniest baby, Mrs. Weymore, you ever looked at—nobody thought he would live. And that would have been a pity, you know; for then the Thetford estate would have gone to a distant branch of the family, as it would, too, if Sir Rupert had been a little girl."

She went on up-stairs to the inhabited part of the building, followed by Mrs. Weymore, who seemed to grow more and more agitated with every word the housekeeper said.

"This is Sir Noel's room," said Mrs. Hilliard, in an awe-struck whisper, as if the dead man still lay there; "no one ever enters here but me."

She unlocked it as she spoke, and went in. Mrs. Weymore followed, with a face of frightened pallor that struck even the housekeeper.

"Good gracious me! Mrs. Weymore, what is the matter? You are as pale as a ghost. Are you afraid to enter a room where a person has died?"

Mrs. Weymore's reply was almost inaudible; she stood on the threshold, pallid, trembling, unaccountably moved. The housekeeper glanced at her suspiciously.

"Very odd," she thought, "very! The new governess is either the most nervous person I ever met, or else—no, she can't have known Sir Noel in his lifetime. Of course not."

They left the chamber after a cursory glance around—Mrs. Weymore never advancing beyond the threshold. She had not spoken, and that white pallor made her face ghastly still.

"I'll show you the picture-gallery," said Mrs. Hilliard; "and then, I believe, you will have seen all that is worth seeing at Thetford Towers."

She led the way to a long, high-lighted room, wainscoted and antique, like all the rest, where long rows of dead and gone Thetfords looked down from the carved walls. There were knights in armor, countesses in ruffles and powder and lace, bishops in mitre on head and crozier in hand, and judges in gown and wig. There were ladies in pointed stomachers and jeweled fans, with the waists of their dresses under their arms, but all fair and handsome, and unmistakably alike. Last of all the long array, there was Sir Noel, a fair-haired, handsome youth of twenty, with a smile on his face and a happy radiance in his blue eyes. And by his side, dark and haughty and beautiful, was my lady in her bridal-robes.

"There is not a handsomer face amongst them all than my lady's," said Mrs. Hilliard, with pride. "You ought to have seen her when Sir Noel first brought her home; she was the most beautiful creature I ever looked at. Ah! it was such a pity he was killed. I suppose they'll be having Sir Rupert's taken next and hung beside her. He don't look much like the Thetfords; he's his mother over again—a Vandeleur, dark and still."

If Mrs. Weymore made any reply the housekeeper did not catch it; she was standing with her face averted, hardly looking at the portraits, and was the first to leave the picture-gallery.

There were a few more rooms to be seen—a drawing-room suite, now closed and disused; an ancient library, with a wonderful stained window, and a vast echoing reception-room. But it was all over at last, and Mrs. Hilliard, with her keys, trotted cheerfully off; and Mrs. Weymore was left to solitude and her own thoughts once more.

A strange person, certainly. She locked the door and fell down on her knees by the bedside, sobbing until her whole form was convulsed.

"Oh! why did I come here? Why did I come here?" came passionately with the wild storm of sobs. "I might have known how it would be! Nearly nine years—nine lone, long years, and not to have forgotten yet!"

CHAPTER V.

A JOURNEY TO LONDON.

Very slowly, very monotonously went life at Thetford Towers. The only noticable change and that my lady went rather more into society, and a greater number of visitors came to the manor. There had been a children's party on the occasion of Sir Rupert's eighth birthday, and Mrs. Weymore had played for the little people to dance; and my lady had cast off her chronic gloom, had been handsome and happy as of old. There had been a dinner-party later—an impreceented event now at Thetford Towers; and the weeds, worn so long, had been discarded, and in diamonds and black velvet Lady Ada Thetford had been beautiful, and stately, and gracious, as a young queen. No one knew the reason of the sudden change, but they accepted the fact just as they found it, and set it down, perhaps, to woman's caprice.

So slowly the summer passed: autumn came and went, and it was December, and the ninth anniversary of Sir Noel's death.

A gloomy day—wet, and wild, and windy. The wind, sweeping over the angry sea, surged and roared through the skeleton trees; the rain lashed the windows in rattling gusts; and the leaden sky hung low and frowning over the drenched and dreary earth. A dismal day—very like that other, nine years ago, that had been Sir Noel's last.

In Lady Thetford's boudoir a bright-red coal fire blazed. Pale-blue curtains of satin damask shut out the wintry prospect, and the softest and richest of foreign carpets hushed every footfall. Before the fire, on a little table, my lady's breakfast temptingly stood; the silver, old and quaint; the rare antique porcelain sparkling in the ruddy firelight. An easy chair, carved and gilded, and cushioned in azure velvet, stood by the table; and near my lady's plate lay the letters and papers the morning's mail had brought.

A toy of a clock on the low marble mantle chimed musically ten as my lady entered. In her dainty morning negligée, with her dark hair rippling and falling low on her neck, she looked very young, and fair, and graceful. Behind her came her maid, a blooming English girl, who took off the cover and poured out my lady's chocolate.

Lady Thetford sank languidly into the azure velvet depths of her *fautenuil*, and took up her letters. There were three—one a note from her man of business; one an invitation to a dinner-party; and the third, a big official-looking document, with a huge seal, and no end of postmarks. The languid eyes suddenly lighted; the pale cheeks flushed as she took it eagerly up. It was a letter from India from Capt. Everard.

Lady Thetford sipped her chocolate, and read her letter leisurely, with her slippered feet on the shining fender. It was a long letter, and she read it over slowly twice, three times, before she laid it down. She finished her breakfast, motioned her maid to remove the service, and lying back in her chair, with her deep, dark eyes fixed dreamily on the fire, she fell into a reverie of other days far gone. The lover of her girlhood came back to her from over the sea. He was lying at her feet once more in the long summer days, under the waving trees of her girlhood's home. Ah, how happy! how happy she had been in those by-gone days, before Sir Noel Thetford had come, with his wealth and his title, to tempt her from her love and truth.

Eleven struck, twelve from the musical clock on the mantle, and still my lady sat living in the past. Outside the wintry storm raged on; the rain clamored against the curtained glass, and the wind worried the trees. With a long sigh my lady awoke from her dream, and mechanically took up the *Times* newspaper—the first of the little heap.

"Vain! vain!" she thought, dreamily; "worse than vain those dreams now. With my own hand I threw back the heart that loved me; of my own free will I resigned the man I loved. And now the old love, that I thought would die in the splendor of my new life, is stronger than ever—and it is nine years too late."

She tried to wrench her thoughts away and fix them on her newspaper. In vain! her eyes wandered aimlessly over the closely-printed columns—her mind was in India with Capt. Everard. All at once she started, uttered a sudden, sharp cry, and grasped the paper with dilated eyes and whitening cheeks. At the top of a column of "personal" advertisements was one which her strained eyes literally devoured.

> "If Mr. Vyking, who ten years ago left a male infant in charge of Mrs. Martha Brand, wishes to keep that child out of the work-house, he will call, within the next five days, at No. 17 Wadington Street, Lambeth."

Again and again, and again Lady Thetford read this apparently uninteresting advertisement. Slowly the paper dropped into her lap, and she sat staring blankly into the fire.

"At last!" she thought, "at last it has come. I fancied all danger was over—the death, perhaps, had forestalled me; and now, after all these years, I am summoned to keep my broken promise!"

The hue of death had settled on her face; she sat cold and rigid, staring with that blank, fixed gaze into the fire. Ceaselessly beat the rain; wilder grew the December day; steadily the moments wore on, and still she sat in that fixed trance. The armula clock struck two—the sound aroused her at last.

"I must!" she said, setting her teeth. "I will! My boy shall not lose his birthright, come what may!"

She rose and rang the bell—very pale, but icily calm. Her maid answered the summons.

"Eliza," my lady asked, "at what hour does the afternoon train leave St. Gosport for London!"

Eliza stared—did not know, but would ascertain. In five minutes she was back.

"At half-past three, my lady; and another at seven."

Lady Thetford glanced at the clock—it was a quarter past two.

"Tell William to have the carriage at the door at a quarter past three; and do you pack my dressing case, and the few things I shall need for two or three days' absence. I am going to London."

Eliza stood for a moment quite petrified. In all the nine years of her service under my lady, no such order as this had ever been received. To go to London at a moment's notice—my lady, who rarely went beyond her own park gates! Turning away, not quite certain that her ears had not deceived her, my lady's voice arrested her.

"Send Mrs. Weymore to me; and do you lose no time in packing up."

Eliza departed. Mrs. Weymore appeared. My lady had some instructions to give concerning the children during her absence. Then the governess was dismissed, and she was again alone.

Through the wind and rain of the wintry storm, Lady Thetford was driven to the station, in time to catch the three-fifty train to the metropolis. She went unattended; with no message to any one, only saying she would be back in three days at the furthest.

In that dull household, where so few events ever disturbed the stagnant quiet, this sudden journey produced an indescribable sensation. What could have taken my lady to London at a moment's notice? Some urgent reason it must have been to force her out of the gloomy seclusion in which she had buried herself since her husband's death. But, discuss it as they might, they could come no nearer the heart of the mystery.

CHAPTER VI.

GUY.

The rainy December day closed in a rainier night. Another day dawned on the world, sunless, and chilly, and overcast still.

It dawned on London in murky, yellow fog, on sloppy, muddy streets—in gloom and dreariness, and a raw, easterly wind. In the densely populated streets of the district of Lambeth, where poverty huddled in tall, gaunt buildings, the dismal light stole murkily and slowly over the crowded, filthy streets and swarming purlieus.

In a small upper room of a large dilapidated house, this bad December morning, a painter stood at his easel. The room was bare and cold, and comfortless in the extreme; the painter was middle-aged, small, brown and shriveled, and very much out at elbows. The dull, gray light fell full on his work—no inspiration of genius by any means—only the portrait, coarsely colored, of a fat, well-to-do butcher's daughter round the corner. The man was Joseph Legard, scene-painter to one of the minor city theatres, who eked out his slender income by painting portraits when he could get them to paint. He was as fond of his art as any of the great, old masters; but he had only one attribute in common with those immortals—extreme poverty; for his salary was not large, and Mr. Legard found it a tight fit, indeed, to "make both ends meet."

So he stood over his work this dull morning, however, in his fireless room, with a cheerful, brown face, whistling a tune. In the adjoining room he could hear his wife's voice raised shrilly, and the cries of half a dozen Legards. He was used to it, and it did not disturb him; and he painted and whistled cheerily, touching up the butcher's daughter's snub nose and fat cheeks and double chin, until light footsteps came running up-stairs, and the door was flung wide by an impetuous hand. A boy of ten, or thereabouts, came in—a bright-eyed, fair-haired lad, with a handsome, resolute face, and eyes of cloudless, Saxon blue.

"Ah, Guy!" said the scene-painter, turning round and nodding good-humoredly. "I've been expecting you! What do you think of Miss Jenkins?"

The boy looked at the picture with the glance of an embryo connoisseur.

"It's as like her as two peas, Joe; or would be, if her hair was a little redder, and her nose a little thicker, and the freckles were plainer. But it looks like her as it is."

"Well, you see, Guy," said the painter, going on with Miss Jenkins's left eyebrow, "it don't do to make 'em too true—people don't like it; they pay their money, and they expect to take it out in good looks. And now, any news this morning, Guy?"

The boy leaned against the window and looked out into the dingy street, his bright, young face growing gloomy and overcast.

"No," he said, moodily; "there is no news, except that Phil Darking was drunk last night, and savage as a mad dog this morning—and that's no news, I'm sure!"

"And nobody's come about the advertisement in the *Times*?"

"No, and never will. It's all humbug what granny says about my belonging to anybody rich; if I did, they'd have seen after me long ago. Phil says my mother was a house-maid, and my father a valet—and they were only too glad to get me off their hands. Vyking was a valet, granny says she knows; and it's not likely he'll turn up after all these years. I don't care, I'd rather go to the work-house; I'd rather starve in the streets, than live another week with Phil Darking."

The blue eyes filled with tears, and he dashed them passionately away. The painter looked up with a distressed face.

"Has he been beating you again, Guy?"

"It's no matter—he's a brute! Granny and Ellen are sorry, and do what they can; but that's nothing. I wish I had never been born!"

"It is hard," said the painter, compassionately, "but keep up heart, Guy; if the worst comes, why you can stop here and take pot-luck with the rest— not that that's much better than starvation. You can take to my business shortly, now; and you'll make a better scene-painter than ever I could. You've got it in you."

"Do you really think so, Joe?" cried the boy, with sparkling eyes. "Do you? I'd rather be an artist than a king——Halloo!"

He stopped short in surprise, staring out of the window. Legard looked. Up the dirty street came a handsome cab, and stopped at their own door. The driver alighted, made some inquiry, then opened the cab-door, and a lady stepped lightly out on the curb-stone—a lady, tall and stately, dressed in black and closely veiled.

"Now, who can this visitor be for?" said Legard. "People in this neighborhood ain't in the habit of having morning calls made on them in cabs. She's coming up-stairs!"

He held the door open, listening. The lady ascended the first flight of stairs, stopped on the landing, and inquired of some one for "Mrs. Martha Brand."

"For granny!" exclaimed the boy. "Joe, I shouldn't wonder if it was some one about that advertisement, after all!"

"Neither should I," said Legard. "There! she's gone in. You'll be sent for directly, Guy!"

Yes, the lady had gone in. She had encountered on the landing a sickly young woman with a baby in her arms, who had stared at the name she inquired for.

"Mrs. Martha Brand? Why, that's mother! Walk in this way, if you please, ma'am."

She opened the door, and ushered the veiled lady into a small, close room, poorly furnished. Over a smouldering fire, mending stockings, sat an old woman, who, notwithstanding the extreme shabbiness and poverty of her dress, lifted a pleasant, intelligent old face.

"A lady to see you, mother," said the young woman, hushing her fretful baby and looking curiously at the veiled face.

But the lady made no attempt to raise the envious screen, not even when Mrs. Martha Brand got up, dropping a respectful little servant's courtesy and placing a chair. It was a very thick veil—an impenetrable shield—and nothing could be discovered of the face behind it but that it was fixedly pale. She sank into the seat, her face turned to the old woman behind that sable screen.

"You are Mrs. Brand?"

The voice was refined and patrician. It would have told she was a lady, even if the rich garments she wore did not.

"Yes, ma'am—your ladyship; Martha Brand."

"And you inserted that advertisement in the *Times* regarding a child left in your care ten years ago?"

Mother and daughter started, and stared at the speaker.

"It was addressed to Mr. Vyking, who left the child in your charge, by which I infer you are not aware that he has left England."

"Left England, has he?" said Mrs. Brand. "More shame for him, then, never to let me know or leave a farthing to support the boy!"

"I am inclined to believe it was not his fault," said the clear, patrician voice. "He left England suddenly and against his will, and, I have reason to think, will never return. But there are others interested—more interested than he could possibly be—in the child, who remain, and who are willing to take him off your hands. But first, why is it you are so anxious, after keeping him all these years, to get rid of him?"

"Well, you see, your ladyship," replied Martha Brand, "it is not me, nor likewise Ellen there, who is my daughter. We'd keep the lad and welcome, and share the last crust we had with him, as we often have—for we're very poor people; but, you see, Ellen, she's married now, and her husband never could bear Guy—that's what we call him, your ladyship—Guy, which it was Mr. Vyking's own orders. Phil Darking, her husband, never did like him somehow; and when he gets drunk, saving your ladyship's presence, he beats him most unmercifully. And now we're going to America—to New York, where Phil's got a brother and work is better, and he won't fetch Guy. So, your ladyship, I thought I'd try once more before we deserted him, and put that advertisement in the *Times*, which I'm very glad I did, if it will fetch the poor lad any friends."

There was a moment's pause; then the lady asked, thoughtfully: "And when do you leave for New York?"

"The day after to-morrow, ma'am—and a long journey it is for a poor old body like me."

"Did you live here when Mr. Vyking left the child with you—in this neighborhood?"

"Not in this neighborhood, nor in London at all, your ladyship. It was Lowdean, in Berkshire, and my husband was alive at the time. I had just lost my baby, and the landlady of the hotel recommended me. So he brought it, and paid me thirty sovereigns, and promised me thirty more every twelvemonth, and told me to call it Guy Vyking—and that was the last I ever saw of him."

"And the infant's mother?" said the lady, her voice changing perceptibly—"do you know anything of her?"

"But very little," said Martha Brand, shaking her head. "I never set eyes on her, although she was sick at the inn for upward of three weeks. But Mrs. Vine, the landlady, she saw her twice; and she told me what a pretty young creeter she was—and a lady, if there ever was a lady yet."

"Then the child was born in Berkshire—how was it?"

"Well, your ladyship, it was an accident, seeing as how the carriage broke down with Mr. Vyking and the lady, a-driving furious to catch the last

London train. The lady was so hurted that she had to be carried to the inn, and went quite out of her head, raving and dangerous like. Mr. Vyking had the landlady to wait upon her until he could telegraph to London for a nurse, which one came down next day and took charge of her. The baby wasn't two days old when he brought it to me, and the poor young mother was dreadful low and out of her head all the time. Mr. Vyking and the nurse were all that saw her, and the doctor, of course; but she didn't die, as the doctor thought she would, but got well, and before she came right to her senses Mr. Vyking paid the doctor and told him he needn't come back. And then, a little more than a fortnight after, they took her away, all sly and secret-like, and what they told her about her poor baby I don't know. I always thought there was something dreadful wrong about the whole thing."

"And this Mr. Vyking—was he the child's father—the woman's husband?"

Martha Brand looked sharply at the speaker, as if she suspected *she* could answer that question best herself.

"Nobody knew, but everybody thought who. I've always been of opinion myself that Guy's father and mother were gentlefolks, and I always shall be."

"Does the boy know his own story?"

"Yes, your ladyship—all I've told you."

"Where is he? I should like to see him."

Mrs. Brand's daughter, all this time hushing her baby, started up.

"I'll fetch him. He's up-stairs in Legard's, I know."

She left the room and ran up-stairs. The painter, Legard, still was touching up Miss Jenkins, and the bright-haired boy stood watching the progress of that work of art.

"Guy! Guy!" she cried breathlessly, "come down-stairs at once. You're wanted."

"Who wants me, Ellen?"

"A lady, dressed in the most elegant and expensive mourning—a real lady, Guy; and she has come about that advertisement, and she wants to see you."

"What is she like, Mrs. Darking?" inquired the painter—"young or old?"

"Young, I should think; but she hides her face behind a thick veil, as if she didn't want to be known. Come, Guy."

She hurried the lad down-stairs and into their little room. The veiled lady still sat talking to the old woman, her back to the dim daylight, and that disguising veil still down. She turned slightly at their entrance, and looked at the boy through it. Guy stood in the middle of the floor, his fearless blue eyes fixed on the hidden face. Could he have seen it he might have started at the grayish pallor which overspread it at sight of him.

"So like! So like!" the lady was murmuring between her set teeth. "It is terrible—it is marvelous!"

"This is Guy, your ladyship," said Martha Brand. "I've done what I could for him for the last ten years, and I'm almost as sorry to part with him as if he were my own. Is your ladyship going to take him away with you now?"

"No," said her ladyship, sharply; "I have no such intention. Have you no neighbor or friend who would be willing to take and bring him up, if well paid for the trouble? This time the money shall be paid without fail."

"There's Legard's," cried the boy, eagerly. "I'll go to Legard's, granny. I'd rather be with Joe than anywhere else."

"It's a neighbor that lives up-stairs," murmured Martha, in explanation. "He always took to Guy and Guy to him in a way that's quite wonderful. He's a very decent man, your ladyship—a painter for a theatre; and Guy takes kindly to the business, and would like to be one himself. If you don't want to take away the boy, you couldn't leave him in better hands."

"I am glad to hear it. Can I see the man?"

"I'll fetch him!" cried Guy, and ran out of the room. Two minutes later came Mr. Legard, paper cap and shirt-sleeves, bowing very low to the grand, black-robed lady, and only too delighted to strike a bargain. The lady offered liberally; Mr. Legard closed with the offer at once.

"You will clothe him better, and you will educate him and give him your name. I wish him to drop that of Vyking. The same amount I give you now will be sent you this time every year. If you change your residence in the meantime, or wish to communicate with me on any occurrence of consequence, you can address Madam Ada, post office, Plymouth."

She rose as she spoke, stately and tall, and motioned Mr. Legard to withdraw. The painter gathered up the money she laid on the table, and bowed himself, with a radiant face, out of the room.

"As for you," turning to old Martha, and taking out of her purse a roll of crisp, Bank of England notes, "I think this will pay you for the trouble you have had with the boy during the last ten years. No thanks—you have earned the money."

She moved to the door, made a slight, proud gesture with her gloved hand in farewell, took a last look at the golden haired, blue eyed, handsome boy, and was gone. A moment later and her cab rattled out of the murky street, and the trio were alone staring at one another, and at the bulky roll of notes.

"I should think it was a dream only for this," murmured old Martha, looking at the roll with glistening eyes. "A great lady—a great lady, surely! Guy, I shouldn't wonder if that was your mother."

CHAPTER VII.

COLONEL JOCYLN.

Five miles away from Thetford Towers, where the multitudinous waves leaped and glistened all day in the sun-light, as if a-glitter with diamonds, stood Jocyln Hall. An imposing structure of red brick, not yet one hundred years old, with sloping meadows spreading away into the blue horizon, and densely wooded plantations gliding down to the wide sea.

Colonel Jocyln, the lord of the boundless meadows and miles of woodland, where the red deer disported in the green arcades, was absent in India, and had been for the past nine years. They were an old family, the Jocylns, as old as any in Devon, and with a pride that bore no proportion to their purse, until the present Jocyln, had, all at once become a millionaire. A penniless young lieutenant in a cavalry regiment, quartered somewhere in Ireland, with a handsome face and dashing manners, he had captivated, at first sight, a wild, young Irish heiress of fabulous wealth and beauty. It was a love-match on her side—nobody knew exactly what it was on his; but they made a moonlight flitting of it, for the lady's friends were grievously wroth. Lieutenant Jocyln liked his profession for its own sake, and took his Irish bride to India, and there an heiress and only child was born to him. The climate disagreed with the young wife—she sickened and died; but the young officer and his baby girl remained in India. In the fullness of time he became Colonel Jocyln; and one day electrified his housekeeper by a letter announcing his intention of returning to England with his little daughter Aileen for good.

That same month of December, which took Lady Thetford on that mysterious London journey, brought this letter from Calcutta. Five months after, when the May primroses and hyacinths were all abloom in the green seaside woodlands, Colonel Jocyln and his little daughter came home.

Early on the day succeeding his arrival, Colonel Jocyln rode through the bright spring sunshine, along the pleasant high road between Jocyln Hall and Thetford Towers. He had met the late Sir Noel and his bride once or twice previous to his departure for India; but there had been no acquaintance sufficiently close to warrant this speedy call.

Lady Thetford, sitting alone in her boudoir, looked in surprise at the card the servant brought.

"Colonel Jocyln," she said, "I did not even know he had arrived. And to call so soon—ah! perhaps he fetches me letters from India."

She rose at the thought, her pale cheeks flushing a little with expectation. Mail after mail had arrived from that distant land, bringing her no letter from Captain Everard.

Lady Thetford descended at once. She had few callers; but she was always exquisitely dressed and ready to receive at a moment's notice. Colonel Jocyln—tall and sallow and soldierly—rose at her entrance.

"Lady Thetford? Ah, yes! Most happy to see your ladyship once more. Permit me to apologize for this very early call—you will overlook my haste when you hear my reason."

Lady Thetford held out her white hand.

"Allow me to welcome you back to England, Colonel Jocyln. You have come for good this time, I hope. And little Aileen is well, I trust?"

"Very well, and very glad to be released from shipboard. I need not ask for young Sir Rupert—I saw him with his nurse in the park as I rode up. A fine boy, and like you, my lady."

"Yes, Rupert is like me. And now—how are our mutual friends in India?"

The momentous question she had been longing to ask from the first; but her well-trained voice spoke it as steadily as though it had been a question of the weather.

Colonel Jocyln's face clouded, darkened.

"I bring bad news from India, my lady. Captain Everard was a friend of yours?"

"Yes; he left his little daughter in my charge."

"I know. You have not heard from him lately?"

"No, and I have been rather anxious. Nothing has befallen the captain, I hope?"

The well-trained voice shook a little despite its admirable training, and the slender fingers looped and unlooped nervously her watch-chain.

"Yes, Lady Thetford; the very worst that could befall him. George Everard is dead."

There was a blank pause. Colonel Jocyln looked grave and downcast and sad.

"He was my friend," he said, in a low voice, "my intimate friend for many years—a fine fellow and brave as a lion. Many, many nights we have lain with the stars of India shining on our bivouac whilst he talked to me of you, of England, of his daughter."

Lady Thetford never spoke, never stirred. She was sitting gazing steadfastly out of the window at the sparkling sunshine, and Colonel Jocyln could not see her face.

"He was as glorious a soldier as ever I knew," the colonel went on; "and he died a soldier's death—shot through the heart. They buried him out there with military honors, and some of his men cried on his grave like children."

There was another blank pause. Still Lady Thetford sat with that fixed gaze on the brilliant May sunshine, moveless as stone.

"It is a sad thing for his poor little girl," the Indian officer said; "she is fortunate in having such a guardian as you, Lady Thetford."

Lady Thetford awoke from her trance. She had been in a trance, and the years had slipped backward, and she had been in her far-off girlhood's home, with George Everard, her handsome, impetuous lover, by her side. She had loved him then, even when she said no and married another; she loved him still, and now he was dead—dead! But she turned to her visitor with a face that told nothing.

"I am so sorry—so very, very sorry. My poor little May! Did Captain Everard speak of her, of me, before he died?"

"He died instantaneously, my lady. There was no time."

"Ah, no! poor fellow! It is the fortune of war—but it is very sad."

That was all; we may feel inexpressibly, but we can only utter commonplaces. Lady Thetford was very, very pale, but her pallor told nothing of the dreary pain at her heart.

"Would you like to see little May? I will send for her."

Little May was sent for and came. A brilliant little fairy as ever, brightly dressed, with shimmering golden curls and starry eyes. By her side stood Sir Rupert—the nine-year-old baronet, growing tall very fast, pale and slender still, and looking at the colonel with his mother's dark, deep eyes.

Colonel Jocyln held out his hand to the flaxen-haired fairy.

"Come here, little May, and kiss papa's friend. You remember papa, don't you?"

"Yes," said May, sitting on his knee contentedly. "Oh, yes! When is papa coming home? He said in mamma's letter he would fetch me lots and lots of dolls and picture-books. Is he coming home?"

"Not very soon," the colonel said, inexpressibly touched; "but little May will go to papa some day. You and mamma, I suppose?" smiling at Lady Thetford.

"Yes," nodded May, "that's mamma, and Rupert's mamma. Oh! I am so sorry papa isn't coming home soon! Do you know"—looking up in his face with big, shining, solemn eyes—"I've got a pony, and I can ride lovely; and his name is Snowdrop, because it's all white; and Rupert's is black, and *his* name is Sultan? And I've got a watch; mamma gave it to me last Christmas; and my doll's name—the big one, you know, that opens its eyes and says 'mamma' and 'papa'—is Sonora. Have you got any little girls at home?"

"One, Miss Chatterbox."

"What's her name!"

"Aileen—Aileen Jocyln."

"Is she nice?"

"Very nice, I think."

"Will she come to see me?"

"If you wish it and mamma wishes it."

"Oh, yes! you do, don't you, mamma? How big is your little girl—as big as me?"

"Bigger, I fancy. She is nine years old."

"Then she's as big as Rupert—*he's* nine years old. May she fetch her doll to see Sonora?"

"Certainly—a regiment of dolls, if she wishes."

"Can't she come to-morrow?" asked Rupert. "To-morrow's May's birthday; May's seven years old to-morrow. Mayn't she come!"

"That must be as mamma says."

"Oh, fetch her!" cried Lady Thetford, "it will be so nice for May and Rupert. Only I hope little May won't quarrel with her; she does quarrel with her playmates a good deal, I am sorry to say."

"I won't if she's nice," said May; "it's all their fault. Oh, Rupert! there's Mrs. Weymore on the lawn, and I want her to come and see the rabbits. There's

- 42 -

five little rabbits this morning, mamma—mayn't I go and show them to Mrs. Weymore?"

Lady Thetford nodded smiling acquiescence; and away ran little May and Rupert to show the rabbits to the governess.

Col. Jocyln lingered for half an hour or upward, conversing with his hostess, and rose to take his leave at last, with the promise of returning on the morrow with his little daughter, and dining at the house. As he mounted his horse and rode homeward, "a haunting shape, an image gay," followed him through the genial May sunshine—Lady Ada Thetford, fair, and stately and graceful.

"Nine years a widow," he mused. "They say she took her husband's death very hard—and no wonder, considering how he died; but nine years is a tolerable time in which to forget. She took the news of Everard's death very quietly. I don't suppose there was ever anything really in that old story. How handsome she is, and how graceful!"

He broke off in his musing fit to light a cigar, and see through the curling smoke dark-eyed Ada, mamma to little Aileen as well as the other two. He had never thought of wanting a wife before, in all these years of his widowhood; but the want struck him forcibly now.

"And Aileen wants a mother, and the little baronet a father," he thought, complacently; "my lady can't do better."

So next day at the earliest possible hour, came back the gallant colonel, and with him a brown-haired, brown-eyed, quiet-looking little girl, as tall, every inch, as Sir Rupert. A little embryo patrician, with pride in her infantile lineaments already, an uplifted poise of the graceful head, a light, elastic step, and a softly-modulated voice. A little lady from top to toe, who opened her little brown eyes in wide wonder at the antics, and gambols, and obstreperousness, generally, of little May.

There were two or three children from the rectory, and half a dozen from other families in the neighborhood—and the little birthday feast was under the charge of Mrs. Weymore, the governess, pale and pretty, and subdued as of old. They raced through the leafy arcades of the park, and gamboled in the garden, and had tea in a fairy summer house, to the music of plashing fountains—and little May was captain of the band. Even shy, still Aileen Jocyln forgot her youthful dignity, and raced and laughed with the best.

"It was so nice, papa!" she cried rapturously, riding home in the misty moonlight. "I never enjoyed myself so well. I like Rupert so much—better than May, you know; May's so rude and laughs so loud. I've asked them to come and see me, papa; and May said she would make her mamma let them come next week. And then I'm going back—I shall always like to go there."

Col. Jocyln smiled as he listened to his little daughter's prattle. Perhaps he agreed with her; perhaps he, too, liked to go there. The dinner-party, at which he and the rector of St. Gosport, and the rector's wife were the only guests, had been quite as pleasant as the birthday fete. Very graceful, very fair and stately, had looked the lady of the manor, presiding at her own dinner-table. How well she would look at the head of his.

The Indian officer, after that, became a very frequent guest at Thetford Towers—the children were such a good excuse. Aileen was lonely at home, and Rupert and May were always glad to have her. So papa drove her over nearly every day, or else came to fetch the other two to Jocyln Hall. Lady Thetford was ever most gracious, and the colonel's hopes ran high.

Summer waned. It was October, and Lady Thetford began talking of leaving St. Gosport for a season; her health was not good, and change of air was recommended.

"I can leave my children in charge of Mrs. Weymore," she said. "I have every confidence in her; and she has been with me so long. I think I shall depart next week; Dr. Gale says I have delayed too long."

Col. Jocyln looked up uneasily. They were sitting alone together, looking at the red October sunset blazing itself out behind the Devon hills.

"We shall miss you very much," he said, softly. "I shall miss you."

Something in his tone struck Lady Thetford. She turned her dark eyes upon him in surprise and sudden alarm. The look had to be answered; rather embarrassed, and not at all so confident as he thought he would have been, Col. Jocyln asked Lady Thetford to be his wife.

There was a blank pause. Then,

"I am very sorry, Col. Jocyln, I never thought of this."

He looked at her, pale—alarmed.

"Does that mean no, Lady Thetford?"

"It means no, Col. Jocyln. I have never thought of you save as a friend; as a friend I still wish to retain you. I will never marry. What I am to-day I will go to my grave. My boy has my whole heart—there is no room in it for anyone else. Let us be friends, Col. Jocyln," holding out her white jeweled hand, "more, no mortal man can ever be to me."

CHAPTER VIII.

LADY THETFORD'S BALL.

Years came and years went, and thirteen passed away. In all these years with their countless changes, Thetford Towers had been a deserted house. Comparatively speaking, of course; Mrs. Weymore, the governess, Mrs. Hilliard, the housekeeper, Mr. Jarvis, the butler, and their minor satellites, served there still, but its mistress and her youthful son had been absent. Only little May had remained under Mrs. Weymore's charge until within the last two years, and then she, too, had gone to Paris to a finishing school.

Lady Thetford came herself to the Towers to fetch her—the only time in these thirteen years. She had spent them pleasantly enough, rambling about the Continent, and in her villa on the Arno, for her health was frail, and growing daily frailer, and demanded a sunny Southern clime. The little baronet had gone to Eton, thence to Oxford, passing his vacation abroad with his mamma—and St. Gosport had seen nothing of them. Lady Thetford had thought it best, for many reasons, to leave little May quietly in England during her wanderings. She missed the child, but she had every confidence in Mrs. Weymore. The old aversion had entirely worn away, but time had taught her she could trust her implicitly; and though May might miss "mamma" and Rupert, it was not in that flighty fairy's nature to take their absence very deeply to heart.

Jocyln Hall was vacated, too. After that refusal of Lady Thetford, Col. Jocyln had left England, placed his daughter in a school abroad, and made a tour of the East.

Lady Thetford he had not met until within the last year, when Lady Thetford and her son, spending the winter in Rome, had encountered Col. and Miss Jocyln, and they had scarcely parted company since. The Thetfords were to return early in the spring to take up their abode once more in the old home, and Col. Jocyln announced his intention of following their example.

Lady Thetford wrote to Mrs. Weymore, her vice-roy, and to her steward, issuing her orders for the expected return. Thetford Towers was to be completely rejuvenated—new furnished, painted and decorated. Landscape gardeners were set at work in the grounds; all things were to be ready the following June.

Summer came and brought the absentees—Lady Thetford and her son, Col. Jocyln and his daughter; and there were bonfires and illuminations, and feasting of tenantry, and ringing of bells, and general jubilation, that the heir of Thetford Towers had come to reign at last.

The week following the arrival, Lady Thetford issued invitations over half the country for a grand ball. Thetford Towers, after over twenty years of gloom and solitude, was coming out again in the old gayety and brilliance that had been its normal state before the present heir was born.

The night of the ball came, and with nearly every one who had been honored with an invitation, all curious to see the future lord of one of the noblest domains in broad Devonshire.

Sir Rupert Thetford stood by his mother's side, and met her old friends for the first time since his boyhood—a slender young man, pale and dark, and handsome of face with dreamy slumbrous eyes of darkness, and quiet manners, not at all like his father's fair-haired, bright-eyed, stalwart Saxon race; the Thetford blood had run out, he was his own mother's son.

Lady Thetford grown pallid and wan, and wasted in all these years, and bearing within the seeds of an incurable disease, looked yet fair and gracious, and stately in her trailing robes and jewels, to-night, receiving her guests like a queen. It was the triumph of her life, the desire of her heart, this seeing her son, her idol, reigning in the home of his fathers, ruler of the broad domain that had owned the Thetfords lord for more years back than she could count.

"If I could but see her his wife," Lady Thetford thought, "I think I should have nothing left on earth to desire."

She glanced across the wide room, along a vista of lights, and flitting forms, and rich dresses, and sparkling jewels, to where a young lady stood, the center of an animated group—a tall and eminently handsome girl, with a proud patrician face, and the courtly grace of a young empress—Aileen Jocyln, heiress of fabulous wealth, possessor of fabulous beauty, and descendant of a race as noble and as ancient as his own.

"With her for his wife, come what might in the future, my Rupert would be safe," the mother thought; "and who knows what a day may bring forth? Ah! if I dared only speak, but I dare not; it would ruin all. I know my son."

Yes, Lady Thetford knew her son, understood his character thoroughly, and was a great deal too wary a conspirator to let him see her cards. Fate, not she, had thrown the heiress and the baronet constantly together of late, and Aileen's own beauty and grace was surely sufficient for the rest. It was the one desire of Lady Thetford's heart; but she never said to her son, who loved her dearly, and would have done a great deal to add to her happiness. She left it to fate, and leaving it, was doing the wisest thing she could possibly do.

It seemed as if her hopes were likely to be realized. Sir Rupert had an artist's and a Sybarite's love for all things beautiful, and could appreciate the grand statuesque style of Miss Jocyln's beauty, even as his mother could not appreciate it. She was like the Pallas Athine, she was his ideal woman, fair and proud, uplifted and serene, smiling on all, from the heights of high-and-mightydom, but shining upon them, a brilliant far-off star, keeping her warmth and sweetness all for him. He was an indolent, dreamy Sybarite, this pale young baronet, who liked his rose-leaves unruffled under him, full of artistic tastes and inspirations, and a great deal too lazy ever to carry them into effect. He was an artist, and he had a studio where he began fifty gigantic deeds at once in the way of pictures, and seldom finished one. Nature had intended him for an artist, not country squire; he cared little for riding, or hunting, or fishing, or farming, or any of the things wherein country squires delight; he liked better to lie on the warm grass, with the summer wind stirring in the trees over his head, and smoke his Turkish pipe, and dream the lazy hours away. If he had been born a poor man he might have been a great painter; as it was, he was only an idle, listless, elegant, languid dreamer, and so likely to remain until the end of the chapter.

Lady Thetford's ball was a very brilliant affair, and a famous success. Until far into the gray and dismal dawn, "flute, violin, bassoon," woke sweet echoes in the once ghostly rooms, so long where silence had reigned. Half the county had been invited, and half the county were there; and hosts of pretty, rosy girls, in arcophane and roses, and sparkling jewelry, baited their dainty traps, and "wove becks and nods, and wreathed smiles," for the special delectation of the handsome courtly heir of Thetford Towers.

But the heir of Thetford Towers, with gracious greetings for all, yet walked through the rose strewn pitfalls all secure, whilst the starry face of Aileen Jocyln shone on him in its pale, high-bred beauty. He had not danced much; he had an antipathy to dancing as he had to exertion of any kind, and presently he stood leaning against a slender white column, watching her in a state of lazy admiration. He could see quite as clearly as his mother how eminently proper a marriage with the heiress of Col. Jocyln would be; he knew by instinct, too, how much she desired it; and it was easy enough, looking at her in her girlish pride and beauty, to fancy himself very much in love, and though anything but a coxcomb, Sir Rupert Thetford was perfectly aware of his own handsome face and dreamy artist's eyes, and his fifteen thousand a year, and lengthy pedigree, and had a hazy idea that the handsome Aileen would not say no when he spoke.

"And I'll speak to-night, by Jove!" thought the young baronet, as near being enthusiastic as was his nature, as he watched her, the brilliant center of a brilliant group. "How exquisite she is in her statuesque grace, my peerless Aileen, the ideal of my dreams. I'll ask her to be my wife to-night, or that inconceivable idiot, Lord Gilbert Penryhn, will do it to-morrow."

He sauntered over to the group, not at all insensible to the quick, bright smile and flitting flush with which Miss Jocyln welcomed him.

"I believe this waltz is mine, Miss Jocyln. Very sorry to break upon your *tete-a-tete*, Penryhn, but necessity knows no law."

A moment and they were floating down the whirling tide of the dance, with the wild, melancholy waltz music swelling and sounding, and Miss Jocyln's perfumed hair breathing fragrance around him, and the starry face and dark, dewy eyes downcast a little, in a happy tremor. The cold, still look of fixed pride seemed to melt out of her face, and an exquisite rosy light came and went in its place, and made her too lovely to tell; and Sir Rupert saw and understood it all, with a little complacent thrill of satisfaction.

They floated out of the ball-room into a conservatory of exquisite blossom, where tropic plants of gorgeous hues, and plashing fountains, under the white light of alabaster lamps, made a sort of garden of Eden. There were orange and myrtle trees oppressing the warm air with their sweetness, and through the open French windows came the soft, misty moonlight and the saline wind. There they stopped, looking out of the pale glory of the night, and there Sir Rupert, about to ask the supreme question of his life, and with his heart beginning to plunge against his side, opened conversation with the usual brilliancy in such cases.

"You look fatigued, Miss Jocyln. These grand balls are great bores, after all."

Miss Jocyln laughed frankly. She was of a nature far more impassioned than his, and she loved him; and she felt thrilling through every nerve in her body the prescience of what he was going to say; for all that, being a woman, she had the best of it now.

"I am not at all fatigued," she said; "and I like it. I don't think balls are bores—like this, I mean; but then, to be sure, my experience is very limited. How lovely the night is! Look at the moonlight, yonder, on the sea—a sheet of silvery glory. Does it not recall Sorrento and the exquisite Sorrentine landscape—that moonlight on the sea? Are you not inspired, sir artist?"

She lifted a flitting, radiant glance, a luminous smile, and the star-like face, drooped again—and the white hands took to reckless breaking off sweet sprays of myrtle.

"My inspiration is nearer," looking down at the drooping face. "Aileen——" and there he stopped, and the sentence was never destined to be finished, for a shadow darkened the moonlight, and a figure flitted in like a spirit and stood before them—a fairy figure, in a cloud of rosy drapery, with shimmering golden curls and dancing eyes of turquoise blue.

Aileen Jocyln started back and away from her companion, with a faint, thrilling cry. Sir Rupert, wondering and annoyed, stood staring; and still the fairy figure in the rosy gauze stood, like a nymph in a stage tableau, smiling up in their faces and never speaking. There was a blank pause, a moment's; then Miss Jocyln made one step forward, doubt, recognition, delight, all in her face at once.

"It is—it is!" she cried, "May Everard!"

"May Everard!" Sir Rupert echoed—"little May!"

"At your service, *monsieur*! To think you should have forgotten me so completely in a decade of years. For shame, Sir Rupert Thetford!"

And then she was in Aileen Jocyln's arms, and there was an hiatus filled up with kisses.

"Oh! what a surprise!" Miss Jocyln cried breathlessly. "Have you dropped from the skies? I thought you were in France."

May Everard laughed, the calm, bright laugh of thirteen years ago, as she held up her dimpled cheeks, first one and then the other, to Sir Rupert.

"Did you? So I was, but I ran away."

"Ran away! From school?"

"Something very like it. Oh! how stupid it was, and I couldn't endure it any longer; and I am so crammed with knowledge now that if I held any more I should burst; and so I told them I had to come home; but I was sent for, which was true, you know, for I felt an inward call; and as they were glad to be rid of me, they didn't make much opposition or ask unnecessary questions. And so," folding the fairy hands and nodding her little ringleted head, "here I am."

"But, good heavens!" cried Sir Rupert, aghast, "you never mean to say, May, you have come alone?"

"All alone," said May, with another nod. "I'm used to it, you know; did it last vacation. Came across and spent it with Mrs. Weymore. I don't mind it the least; don't know what sea-sickness is; and oh! didn't some of the poor wretches suffer this time! Isn't it fortunate I'm here for the ball? And, Rupert, good gracious! how you've grown!"

"Thanks. I can't see that you have changed much, Miss Everard. You are the same curly-headed, saucy fairy I knew thirteen years ago. What does my lady say to this escapade?"

"Nothing. Eloquent silence best expresses her feelings; and then she hadn't time to make a scene. Are you going to ask me to dance, Rupert? because if you are," said Miss Everard, adjusting her bracelet, "you had better do it at once, as I am going back to the ball-room, and after I once appear there you will stand no chance amongst the crowd of competitors. But then, perhaps you belong to Miss Jocyln?"

"Not at all," Miss Jocyln interposed, hastily, and reddening a little; "I am engaged, and it is time I was back, or my unlucky cavalier will be at his wit's end to find me."

She swept away with a quicker movement than her wont, and Sir Rupert laughingly gave his piquant little partner his arm. His notions of propriety were a good deal shocked; but then it was only May Everard, and May Everard was one of those exceptionable people who can do pretty much as they please, and not surprise any one. They went back to the ball-room, the fairy in pink on the arm of the young baronet, chattering like a magpie. Miss Jocyln's partner found her and led her off; but Miss Jocyln was very silent and *distrait* all the rest of the night, and watched furtively, but incessantly, the fluttering pink fairy. She had reigned belle hitherto, but sparkling little May, like an embodied sunbeam, electrified the rooms, and took the crown and the sceptre by royal right. Sir Rupert had that one dance, and no more—Miss Everard's own prophecy was true—the demand for her was such that even the son of the house stood not the shadow of a chance.

Miss Jocyln held herself aloof from the young baronet for the remaining hours of the ball. She had known as well as he the words that were on his lips when May Everard interposed, and her eyes flashed and her dark cheek flushed dusky red to see how easily he had been deterred from his purpose. For him, he sought her once or twice in a desultory sort of way, never noticing that he was purposely avoided, wandering contentedly back to devote himself to some one else, and in the pauses to watch May Everard floating—a sunbeam in a rosy cloud—here and there and everywhere.

CHAPTER IX.

GUY LEGARD.

"He meant to have spoken that night; he would have spoken but for May Everard. And yet that is two weeks ago, and we have been together since, and——"

Aileen Jocyln broke off abruptly, and looked out over the far-spreading, gray sea.

The morning was dull, the leaden sky threatening rain, the wind sighing fitfully, and the slow, gray sea creeping up the gray sands. Aileen Jocyln sat as she had sat since breakfast, aimless and dreary, by her dressing-room window, gazing blankly over the pale landscape, her hair falling loose and damp over her shoulders, and a novel lying listlessly in her lap. The book had no interest; her thoughts would stray, in spite of her, to Thetford Towers.

"She is very pretty," Miss Jocyln thought, "with that pink and white wax-doll sort of prettiness some people admire. I never thought *he* could, with his artistic nature; but I suppose I was mistaken. They call her fascinating; I believe that rather hoidenish manner of hers, and all those dashing airs, and that 'loud' style of dress and doings, take some men by storm. I presume I was mistaken in Sir Rupert, I dare say pretty, penniless May will be Lady Thetford before long."

Miss Jocyln's short upper-lip curled rather scornfully, and she rose up with a little air of petulance and walked across the room to the opposite window. It commanded a view of the lawn and a long wooded drive, and, cantering airily up under the waving trees, she saw the young lady of whom she had been thinking. The pretty, fleet-footed pony and his bright little mistress were by no means rare visitors at Jocyln Hall, and Miss Jocyln was always elaborately civil to Miss Everard. Very pretty little May looked—all her tinseled curls floating in the breeze, like a golden banner; the blue eyes more starily radiant than ever, the dark riding-habit and jaunty hat and plume the most becoming things in the world. She saw Miss Jocyln at the window, kissed her hand and resigned Arab to the groom. A minute more and she was saluting Aileen with effusion.

"You solemn Aileen! to sit and mope here in the house, instead of improving your health and temper by a breezy canter over the downs. Don't contradict; I know you were moping. I should be afraid to tell you how many miles Arab and I have got over this morning. And you never came to see me yesterday, either. Why was it?"

"I didn't feel inclined," Miss Jocyln answered, truthfully.

"No, you never *do* feel inclined unless I come and drag you out by force; you sit in the house and grow yellow and jaundiced over high-church novels. I declare I never met so many lazy people in all my life as I have done since I came home. One don't mind mamma, poor thing! shutting herself up and the sunshine and fresh air of heaven out; but, for you and Rupert! And, speaking of Rupert," ran on Miss Everard in a breathless sort of way, "he wanted to commence his great picture of 'Fair Rosamond and Eleanor' yesterday—and how could he when Eleanor never came? Why didn't you—you promised?"

"I changed my mind, I suppose."

"And broke your word—more shame for you, then! Come now."

"No; thanks. It's going to rain."

"Nothing of the sort; and Rupert is *so* anxious. He would have come himself, only my lady is ill to-day with one of her bad headaches, and asked him to read her to sleep; and, like the good boy that he is in the main, though shockingly lazy, he obeyed. Do come, Aileen; there's a dear! Don't be selfish."

Miss Jocyln rose rather abruptly.

"I have no desire to be selfish, Miss Everard. If you will wait ten minutes whilst I dress, I will accompany you to Thetford Towers."

She rang the bell and swept from the room, stately and uplifted. May looked after her, fidgeting a little.

"Dear me! I suppose she's offended now at that word 'selfish.' I never *did* get on very well with Aileen Jocyln, and I'm afraid I never shall. I shouldn't wonder if she were jealous."

Miss Everard laughed a little silvery laugh all to herself, and slapped her kid riding-boot with her pretty toy whip.

"I hope I didn't interrupt a tender declaration that night in the conservatory, but it looked like it. If I did, I am sure Rupert has had fifty chances since, and I know he hasn't availed himself of them, or Aileen would never wear that dissatisfied face. I know she's in love with *him*, though, to be sure, she would see me impaled with the greatest pleasure if she only thought I suspected it; but I'm not so certain about him. He's a great deal too indolent in the first place, to get up a grand passion for anybody, and I think he's inclined to look graciously on me—poor little me—in the second. You may spare yourself the trouble, my dear Sir Rupert; for a gentleman whose chief aim in existence is to smoke Turkish pipes and lie on the grass and write and read poetry is not at all the sort of man I mean to bless for life."

The two girls descended to the court-yard, mounted and rode off. Both rode well, and both looked their best on horseback, and made a wonderfully pretty picture as they galloped through St. Gosport in dashing style, bringing the admiring population in a rush to doors and windows. Perhaps Sir Rupert Thetford thought so, too, as he stood at the great front entrance to receive them, with a kindling light in his artist's eyes.

"May said she would fetch you, and May always keeps her word," he said, as he walked slowly up the sweeping staircase; "besides, Aileen, I am to have the first sitting for the 'Rosamond and Eleanor' to-day, am I not? May calls me an idle dreamer, a useless drone in the busy human hive; so, to vindicate my character and cleave a niche in the temple of fame, I am going to immortalize myself over this painting."

"You'll never finish it," said May; "it will be like all the rest. You'll begin on a gigantic scale and with super-human efforts, and you'll cool down and get sick of it before it is half finished, and it will go to swell the pile of daubed canvas in your studio now. Don't tell me! I know you."

"And have the poorest possible opinion of me, Miss Everard?"

"Yes, I have! I have no patience when I think what you might do, what you might become, and see what you are! If you were not Sir Rupert Thetford, with a princely income, you might be a great man. As it is——"

"As it is!" cried the young baronet, trying to laugh and reddening violently, "I will still be a great man—a modern Murillo. Are you not a little severe, Miss Everard? Aileen, I believe this is your first visit to my studio?"

"Yes," said Miss Jocyln, coldly and briefly. She did not like the conversation, and May Everard's familiar home-truths stung her. To her he was everything mortal man should be; she was proud, but she was not ambitious; what right had this penniless little free-speaker to come between them and talk like this?

May was flitting about like the fairy she was, her head a little on one side, like a critical canary, her flowing skirt held up, inspecting the pictures.

"'Jeanne D'Arc before her Judges,' half finished, as usual, and never to be completed; and weak—very, if it ever *was* completed. 'Battle of Bosworth Field,' in flaming colors, all confusion and smoke and red ochre and rubbish; you did well not to trouble yourself any more with that. 'Swiss

Peasant'—ah! that *is* pretty. 'Storm at Sea,' just tolerable. 'Trial of Marie Antoinette.' My dear Rupert, why will you persist in these figure paintings when you know your forte is landscape? 'An Evening in the Eternal City.' Now, that is what I call an exquisite little thing! Look at the moon, Aileen, rising over those hill-tops; and see those trees—you can almost feel the wind that blows! And that prostrate figure—why, that looks like yourself, Rupert!"

"It *is* myself."

"And the other, stooping—who is he?"

"The painter of that picture, Miss Everard; yes, the only thing in my poor studio you see fit to eulogize is not mine. It was done by an artist friend— an unknown Englishman, who saved my life in Rome three years ago. Come in, mother mine, and defend your son from the two-edged sword of May Everard's tongue."

For Lady Thetford, pale and languid, appeared on the threshold, wrapped in a shawl.

"It's all for his good, mamma. Come here and look at this 'Evening in the Eternal City.' Rupert has nothing like it in all his collection, though these are the beginning of many better things. He saved your life? How was it?"

"Oh! a little affair with brigands; nothing very thrilling, but I should have been killed or captured all the same, if this Legard had not come to the rescue. May is right about the picture; he painted well, had come to Rome to perfect himself in his art. Very fine fellow, Legard."

"Legard!"

It was Lady Thetford who had spoken sharply and suddenly. She had put up her glass to look at the Italian picture, but dropped it, and faced abruptly round.

"Yes, Legard. Guy Legard, a young Englishman, about my own age. By-the-bye, if you saw him, you would be surprised by his singular resemblance to some of those dead and gone Thetfords hanging over there in the picture-gallery—fair hair, blue eyes, and the same peculiar cast of features to a shade. I was rather taken aback, I confess, when I saw it first. My dear mother——"

It was not a cry Lady Thetford had uttered—it was a kind of wordless sob. He soon caught her in his arms and held her there, her face the color of death.

"Get a glass of water, May—she is subject to these attacks. Quick!"

Lady Thetford drank the water, and sunk back in the chair Aileen wheeled up, her face looking awfully corpse-like in contrast to her dark garments and dead black hair.

"You should not have left your room," said Sir Rupert, "after your attack this morning. Perhaps you had better return and lie down. You look perfectly ghastly."

"No," his mother sat up as she spoke and pushed away the glass, "there is no necessity for lying down. Don't wear that scared face, May—it was nothing, I assure you. Go on with what you were saying, Rupert."

"What I was saying? What was it?"

"About this young artist's resemblance to the Thetfords."

"Oh! well, there's no more to say; that is all. He saved my life and he painted that picture, and we were Damon and Pythias over again during my stay in Rome. I always *do* fraternize with those sort of fellows, you know; and I left him in Rome, and he promised, if he ever returned to England— which he wasn't so sure of—he would run down to Devonshire to see me and my painted ancestors, whom he resembles so strongly. That is all; and now, young ladies, if you will take your places we will commence on the Rosamond and Eleanor. Mother, sit here by this window if you want to play propriety, and don't talk."

But Lady Thetford chose to go to her own room, and her son gave her his arm thither and left her lying back amongst her cushions in front of the fire. It was always chilly in those great and somewhat gloomy rooms, and her ladyship was always cold of late. She lay there looking with gloomy eyes into the ruddy blaze, and holding her hands over her painfully beating heart.

"It is destiny, I suppose," she thought, bitterly; "let me banish him to the farthest end of the earth; let me keep him in poverty and obscurity all his life, and when the day comes that it is written, Guy Legard will be here. Sooner or later the vow I have broken to Sir Noel Thetford must be kept; sooner or later Sir Noel's heir will have his own."

CHAPTER X.

ASKING IN MARRIAGE.

A fire burned in Lady Thetford's room, and among piles of silken pillows my lady, languid and pale, lay, looking into the leaping flame. It was a hot July morning, the sun blazed like a wheel of fire in a sky without a cloud, but Lady Thetford was always chilly of late. She drew the crimson shawl she wore closer around her, and glanced impatiently now and then at the pretty toy clock on the decorated chimney-piece. The house was very still; its one disturbing element, Miss Everard, was absent with Sir Rupert for a morning canter over the sunny Devon hills.

"How long they stay, and these solitary rides are so dangerous! Oh! what will become of me if it is too late, after all! What shall I do if he says no?"

There was a quick man's step without—a moment and the door opened, and Sir Rupert, "booted and spurred" from his ride, was bending over his mother.

"Louise says you sent for me after I left. What is it, mother—you are not worse?"

He knelt beside her. Lady Thetford put back the fair brown hair with tender touch, and gazed in the handsome face so like her own, with eyes full of unspeakable love.

"My boy! my boy!" she murmured, "my darling Rupert! Oh! it *is* hard, it *is* bitter to have to leave you!"

"Mother!" with a quick look of alarm, "what is it? Are you worse?"

"No worse, Rupert; but no better. My boy, I shall never be better again in this world."

"Mother——"

"Hush, my Rupert—wait; you know it is true; and but for leaving you I should be glad to go. My life has not been so happy since your father died, that I should greatly cling to it."

"But, mother, this won't do; these morbid fancies are worst of all. Keeping up one's spirits is half the battle."

"I am not morbid; I merely state a fact—a fact which must preface what is to come. Rupert, I know I am dying, and before we part I want to see my successor at Thetford Towers."

"My dear mother!" amazedly.

"Rupert, I want to see Aileen Jocyln your wife. No, no; don't interrupt me, but believe me, I dislike match-making quite as cordially as you do; but my days on earth are numbered, and I must speak before it is too late. When we were abroad I thought there never would be occasion; when we returned home I thought so, too. Rupert, I have ceased to think so since May Everhard's return."

The young man's face flushed suddenly and hotly, but he made no reply.

"How any man in his senses could possibly prefer May to Aileen, is a mystery I cannot solve; but then these things puzzle the wisest of us at times. Mind, my boy, I don't really say you *do* prefer May—I should be very unhappy if I thought so. I know—I am certain you love Aileen best; and I am equally certain she is a thousand times better suited to you. Then, as a man of honor, you owe it to her. You have paid Miss Jocyln such attentions as no honorable gentleman should pay any lady, save the one he means to make his wife."

Lady Thetford's son rose abruptly, and stood leaning against the mantle, looking into the fire.

"Rupert, tell me truly, if May Everard had not come here, would you not ere this have asked Aileen to be your wife?"

"Yes—no—I don't know! Mother!" the young man cried, impatiently, "what has May Everard done that you should treat her like this?"

"Nothing; and I love her dearly, and you know it. But she is not suited to you—she is not the woman you should marry."

Sir Rupert laughed—a hard strident laugh.

"I think Miss Everard is much of your opinion, my lady. You might have spared yourself all these fears and perplexities, for the simple reason that I should have been refused had I asked."

"Rupert?"

"Nay, mother mine, no need to wear that frightened face. I haven't asked Miss Everard in so many words to marry me, and she hasn't declined with thanks; but she would if I did. I saw enough to-day of that."

"Then you don't care for Aileen?" with a look of blank consternation.

"I care for her very much, mother; and I haven't owned to being absolutely in love with our pretty little May. Perhaps I care for one as much as the other; perhaps I know in my inmost heart she is the one I should marry. That is, if she will marry me."

"You owe it to her to ask her."

"Do I? Very likely; and it would make you happy, my mother?"

He came and bent over her again, smiling down in her wan, anxious face.

"More happy than anything else in this world, Rupert!"

"Then consider it an accomplished fact. Before the sun sets to-day Aileen Jocyln shall say yes or no to your son."

He bent and kissed her; then, without waiting for her to speak, wheeled round and strode out of the apartment.

"There is nothing like striking whilst the iron is hot," said the young man to himself, with a grim sort of smile, as he ran down-stairs.

Loitering on the lawn, he encountered May Everard, still in her riding-habit, surrounded by three or four poodle-dogs.

"On the wing again, Rupert? Is it for mamma? She is not worse?"

"No; I am going to Jocyln Hall. Perhaps I shall fetch Aileen back."

May's turquoise blue eyes were lifted with a sudden luminous, intelligent flash to his face.

"God speed you! You will certainly fetch Aileen back!"

She held out her hand with a smile that told him she knew all as plainly as he knew it himself.

"You have my best wishes, Rupert, and don't linger; I want to congratulate Aileen."

Sir Rupert's response to these good wishes was very brief and curt. Miss Everard watched him mount and ride off, with a mischievous little smile rippling round her rosy lips.

"My lady has been giving the idol of her existence a caudle lecture—subject, matrimony," mused Miss Everard, sauntering lazily along in the midst of her little dogs: "and really it is high time, if she means to have Aileen for a daughter-in-law, for the heir of Thetford Towers is rather doubtful that he is not falling in love with me; and Aileen is dreadfully jealous and disagreeable; and my lady is anxious and fidgeted to death about it; and—oh-h-h! good gracious!"

Miss Everard stopped with a shrill, feminine shriek. She had loitered down to the gates, where a young man stood talking to the lodge-keeper, with a big Newfoundland dog gamboling ponderously about him. The big Newfoundland made an instant dash into Miss Everard's guard of honor, with one deep, bass bark, like distant thunder, and which effectually drowned the yelps of the poodles. May flew to the rescue, seizing the Newfoundland's collar and pulling him back with all the might of two little white hands.

"You big, horrid brute!" cried May, with flashing eyes, "how dare you! Call off your dog, sir, this instant! Don't you see how he is frightening mine!"

She turned imperiously to the Newfoundland's master, the bright eyes flashing, the pink cheeks aflame—very pretty, indeed, in her wrath.

"Down, Hector!" called the young man, authoritatively; and Hector, like the well-trained animal he was, subsided instantly. "I beg your pardon, young lady! Hector, you stir at your peril, sir! I am very sorry he has alarmed you."

He doffed his cap with careless grace, and made the angry little lady a courtly bow.

"He didn't alarm me," replied May, testily; "he only alarmed my dogs. Why, dear me! how very odd!"

Miss Everard, looking full at the young man, had started back with this exclamation and stared broadly. A tall, powerful-looking young fellow, rather dusty and travel-stained, but eminently gentlemanly, with frank blue eyes and profuse fair hair, and a handsome, candid face.

"Yes, Miss May," struck in the lodge-keeper, "it is odd! I see it, too! He looks enough like Sir Noel, dead and gone, to be his own son!"

"I beg your pardon," said May, becoming conscious of her wide stare, "but is your name Legard, and are you a friend of Sir Rupert Thetford?"

"Yes, to both questions," with a smile that May liked. "You see the resemblance too, then. Sir Rupert used to speak of it. Is he at home?"

"Not just now; but he will be very soon, and I know will be glad to see Mr. Legard. You had better come in and wait."

"And Hector," said Mr. Legard. "I think I had better leave him behind, as I see him eying your guard of honor with anything but a friendly eye. I believe I have the pleasure of addressing Miss Everard? Oh!" laughing frankly at her surprised face, "Sir Rupert showed me a photograph of yours as a child. I have a good memory for faces, and knew you at once."

Miss Everard and Mr. Legard fell easily into conversation at once, as if they had been old friends. Lady Thetford's ward was one of those people who form their likes and dislikes at first sight, and Mr. Legard's face would have been a pretty sure letter of recommendation to him the wide world over. May liked his looks; and then he was Sir Rupert's friend, and she was never over particular about social forms and customs; and so they dawdled about the grounds and through the leafy arcades, in the genial sunshine, talking about Sir Rupert and Rome, and art and artists, and the thousand and one things that turn up in conversation; and the moments slipped by, half hour followed half hour, until May jerked out her watch at last, in a sudden fit of recollection, and found, to her consternation, it was past two.

"What will mamma say!" cried the young lady, aghast. "And Rupert; I dare say he's home to luncheon before this. Let us go back to the house, Mr. Legard. I had no idea it was half so late."

Mr. Legard laughed frankly.

"The honesty of that speech is the highest flattery my conversational powers ever received, Miss Everard. I am very much obliged to you. Ah! by Jove! Sir Rupert himself!"

For riding slowly up under the sunlit trees came the young baronet. As Mr. Legard spoke, his glance fell upon them, the young lady and gentleman advancing so confidentially with half a dozen curly poodles frisking about them. To say Sir Rupert stared would be a mild way of putting it—his eyes opened in wide wonder.

"Guy Legard!"

"Thetford! My dear Sir Rupert!"

The baronet leaped off his horse, his eyes lighting, and shook hands with the artist, in a burst of heartiness very rare with him.

"Where in the world did you drop from, and how under the sun did you come to be *like this* with May?"

"I leave the explanation to Mr. Legard," said May, blushing a little under Sir Rupert's glance, "whilst I go and see mamma, only premising that luncheon hour is past, and you had better not linger."

She tripped away, and the two young men followed more slowly into the house. Sir Rupert led his friend to his studio, and left him to inspect the pictures.

"Whilst I speak a word to my mother," he said; "it will detain me hardly an instant."

"All right!" said Mr. Legard, boyishly. "Don't hurry yourself on my account, you know."

Lady Thetford lay where her son had left her—lay as if she had hardly stirred since. She looked up and half rose as he came in, her eyes painfully, intensely anxious. But his face, grave and quiet, told nothing.

"Well," she panted, her eyes glittering.

"It is well, mother. Aileen Jocyln has promised to become my wife."

"Thank God!"

Lady Thetford sunk back, her hands clasped tightly over her heart, its loud beating plainly audible. Her son looked down at her, his face keeping its steady gravity—none of the rapture of an accepted lover there.

"You are content, mother?"

"More than content, Rupert. And you?"

He smiled and, stooping, kissed the warm, pallid face. "I would do a great deal to make you happy, mother; but I would *not* ask a woman I did not love to be my wife. Be at rest; all is well with me. And now I must leave you, if you will not go down to luncheon."

"I think not; I am not strong to-day. Is May waiting?"

"More than May. A friend of mine has arrived, and will stay with us for a few weeks."

Lady Thetford's face had been flushed and eager, but at the last words it suddenly blanched.

"A friend, Rupert! Who?"

"You have heard me speak of him before," he said carelessly; "his name is Guy Legard."

CHAPTER XI.

ON THE WEDDING EVE.

The family at Thetford Towers were a good deal surprised, a few hours later that day, by the unexpected appearance of Lady Thetford at dinner. Wan as some spirit of the moonlight, she came softly in, just as they entered the dining-room, and her son presented his friend, Mr. Legard, at once.

"His resemblance to the family will be the surest passport to your favor, mother mine," Sir Rupert said, gayly. "Mrs. Weymore met him just now, and recoiled with a shriek, as though she had seen a ghost. Extraordinary, isn't it—this chance resemblance?"

"Extraordinary," Lady Thetford said, "but not at all unusual. Of course, Mr. Legard is not even remotely connected with the Thetford family?"

She asked the question without looking at him. She kept her eyes fixed on her plate, for that frank, fair face before her was terrible to her, almost as a ghost. It was the days of her youth over again, and Sir Noel, her husband, once more by her side.

"Not that I am aware of," Mr. Legard said, running his fingers through his abundant brown hair. "But I may be for all that. I am like the hero of a novel—a mysterious orphan—only, unfortunately, with no identifying strawberry mark on my arm. Who my parents were, or what my real name is, I know no more than I do of the biography of the man in the moon."

There was a murmur of astonishment—May and Rupert vividly interested, Lady Thetford white as a dead woman her eyes averted, her hand trembling as if palsied.

"No," said Mr. Legard, gravely, and a little sadly, "I stand as totally alone in this world as a human being can stand—father, mother, brother, sister, I never have known; a nameless, penniless waif, I was cast upon the world four-and-twenty years ago. Until the age of twelve I was called Guy Vyking; then the friends with whom I had lived left England for America, and a man—a painter, named Legard—took me and gave me his name. And there the romance comes in: a lady, a tall, elegant lady, too closely veiled for us to see her face, came to the poor home that was mine, paid those who had kept me from my infancy, and paid Legard for his future care of me. I have never seen her since; and I sometimes think," his voice failing, "that she may have been my mother."

There was a sudden clash, and a momentary confusion. My lady, lifting her glass with that shaking hand, had let it fall, and it was shivered to atoms on the floor.

"And you never saw the lady afterward?" May asked.

"Never. Legard received regular remittances, mailed, oddly enough, from your town here—Plymouth. The lady told him, if he ever had occasion to address her—which he never did have, that I know of—to address Madam Ada, Plymouth! He brought me up, educated me, taught me his art and died. I was old enough then to comprehend my position, and the first use I made of that knowledge was to return 'Madam Ada' her remittances, with a few sharp lines that effectually put an end to hers."

"Have you never tried to ferret out the mystery of your birth and this Madam Ada?" inquired Sir Rupert.

Mr. Legard shook his head.

"No; why should I? I dare say I should have no reason to be proud of my parents if I did find them, and they evidently were not very proud of me. 'Where ignorance is bliss,' etc. If destiny has decreed it, I shall know, sooner or later; if destiny has not, then my puny efforts will be of no avail. But if presentiments mean anything, I shall one day know; and I have no doubt, if I searched Devonshire, I should find Madam Ada."

May Everard started up with a cry, for Lady Thetford had fallen back in one of those sudden spasms to which she had lately become subject. In the universal consternation Guy Legard and his story were forgotten.

"I hope what *I* said had nothing to do with this," he cried, aghast; and the one following so suddenly upon the other made the remark natural enough. But Sir Rupert turned upon him in haughty surprise.

"What *you* said! Lady Thetford, unfortunately, has been subject to these attacks for the past two years, Mr. Legard. That will do, May; let me assist my mother to her room."

May drew back. Lady Thetford was able to rise, ghastly and trembling, and, supported by her son's arm, walked from the room.

"Lady Thetford's health is very delicate, I fear," Mr. Legard murmured, sympathetically. "I really thought for a moment my story-telling had occasioned her sudden illness."

Miss Everard fixed a pair of big, shining eyes in solemn scrutiny on his face—that face so like the pictured one of Sir Noel Thetford.

"A very natural supposition," thought the young lady; "so did *I*."

"You never knew Sir Noel?" Guy Legard said, musingly; "but, of course, you did not. Sir Rupert has told me he died before he was born."

"I never saw him," said May; "but those who have seen him in this house— our housekeeper, for instance—stand perfectly petrified at your extraordinary likeness to him. Mrs. Hilliard says you have given her a 'turn' she never expects to get over."

Mr. Legard smiled, but was grave again directly.

"It is odd—odd—very odd!"

"Yes," said May Everard, with a sagacious nod; "a great deal, too, to be a chance resemblance. Hush! here comes Rupert. Well, how have you left mamma?"

"Better; Louise is with her. And now to finish dinner; I have an engagement for the evening."

Sir Rupert was strangely silent and *distrait* all through dinner, a darkly thoughtful shadow glooming his ever pale face. A supposition had flashed across his mind that turned him hot and cold by turns—a supposition that was almost a certainty. This striking resemblance of the painter Legard to his dead father was no freak of nature, but a retributive Providence revealing the truth of his birth. It came back to his memory with painfully acute clearness that his mother had sunk down once before in a violent tremor and faintness at the mere sound of his name. Legard had spoken of a veiled lady—Madam Ada, Plymouth, her address. Could his mother— his—be that mysterious arbiter of his fate? The name—the place. Sir Rupert Thetford wrenched his thoughts, by a violent effort, away, shocked at himself.

"It cannot be—it cannot!" he said to himself passionately. "I am mad to harbor such thoughts. It is a desecration of the memory of the dead, a treason to the living. But I wish Guy Legard had never come here."

There was one other person at Thetford Towers strangely and strongly affected by Mr. Guy Legard, and that person, oddly enough, was Mrs. Weymore, the governess. Mrs. Weymore had never even seen the late Sir Noel that any one knew of, and yet she had recoiled with a shrill, feminine cry of utter consternation at sight of the young man.

"I don't see why you should get the fidgets about it, Mrs. Weymore," Miss Everard remarked, with her great, bright eyes suspiciously keen; "you never knew Sir Noel."

Mrs. Weymore sunk down on a lounge in a violent tremor and faintness.

"My dear, I beg your pardon. I—it seems strange, Oh, May!" with a sudden, sharp cry, losing self-control, "who *is* that young man?"

"Why, Mr. Guy Legard, artist," answered May, composedly, the bright eyes still on the alert; "formerly—in 'boyhood's sunny hours,' you know—Master Guy. Let—me—see! Yes, Vyking."

"Vyking!" with a spasmodic cry; and then Mrs. Weymore dropped her white face in her hands, trembling from head to foot.

"Well, upon my word," Miss Everard said, addressing empty space, "this does cap the globe! The Mysteries of Udolpho were plain reading compared to Mr. Guy Vyking and the effect he produces upon the people. He's a very handsome young man, and a very agreeable young man; but I should never have suspected he possessed the power of throwing all the elderly ladies he meets into gasping fits. There's Lady Thetford: he was too much for her, and she had to be helped out of the dining-room; and here's Mrs. Weymore going into hysterics because he used to be called Guy Vyking. I thought my lady might be the veiled lady of his story; but now I think it must have been you."

Mrs. Weymore looked up, her very lips white.

"The veiled lady? What lady? May, tell me all you know of Mr. Vyking."

"Not Vyking now—Legard," answered May; and there-upon the young lady detailed the scanty *resume* the artist had given them of his history.

"And I'm very sure it isn't chance at all," concluded May Everard, transfixing the governess with an unwinking stare; "and Mr. Legard is as much a Thetford as Sir Rupert himself. I don't pretend to divination, of course, and I don't clearly see how it is; but it is, and you know it, Mrs. Weymore; and you could enlighten the young man, and so could my lady, if either of you chose."

Mrs. Weymore turned suddenly and caught May's two hands in hers.

"May, if you care for me, if you have any pity, don't speak of this. I *do* know—but I must have time. My head is in a whirl. Wait, wait, and don't tell Mr. Legard."

"I won't," said May; "but it is all very strange and very mysterious, delightfully like a three-volume novel or a sensation play. I'm getting very much interested in the hero of the performance, and I'm afraid I shall be deplorably in love with him shortly if this sort of thing keeps on."

Mr. Legard himself took the matter much more coolly than any one else; smoked cigars philosophically, criticised Sir Rupert's pictures, did a little that way himself, played billiards with his host and chess with Miss Everard, rode with that young lady, walked with her, sang duets with her in a deep melodious bass, made himself fascinating, and took the world easy.

"It is no use getting into a gale about these things," he said to Miss Everard when she wondered aloud at his constitutional phlegm; "the crooked things will straighten of themselves if we give them time. What is written is written. I know I shall find out all about myself one day—like little Paul Dombey, 'I feel it in my bones.'"

Mr. Legard was thrown a good deal upon Miss Everard's resources for amusement; for, of course, Sir Rupert's time was chiefly spent at Jocyln Hall, and Mr. Legard bore this with even greater serenity than the other. Miss Everard was a very charming little girl, with a laugh that was sweeter than the music of the spheres and hundreds of bewitching little ways; and Mr. Legard undertook to paint her portrait, and found it the most absorbing work of art he had ever undertaken. As for the young baronet spending his time at Jocyln Hall, they never missed him. His wooing sped on smoothest wings—Col. Jocyln almost as much pleased as my lady herself; and the course of true love in this case ran as smooth as heart could wish.

Miss Jocyln, as a matter of course, was a great deal at Thetford Towers, and saw with evident gratification the growing intimacy of Mr. Legard and May. It would be an eminently suitable match, Miss Jocyln thought, only it was a pity so much mystery shrouded the gentleman's birth. Still, he was a gentleman, and, with his talents, no doubt would become an eminent artist; and it would be highly satisfactory to see May fix her erratic affections on somebody, and thus be doubly out of her—Miss Jocyln's—way.

The wedding preparations were going briskly forward. There was no need of delay; all were anxious for the marriage—Lady Thetford more than anxious, on account of her declining health. The hurry to have the ceremony irrevocably over had grown to be something very like a monomania with her.

"I feel that my days are numbered," she said, with impatience, to her son, "and I cannot rest in my grave, Rupert, until I see Aileen your wife."

So Sir Rupert, more than anxious to please his mother, hastened on the wedding. An eminent physician, summoned down from London, confirmed my lady's own fears.

"Her life hung by a thread," this gentleman said, confidentially to Sir Rupert, "the slightest excitement may snap it at any moment. Don't contradict her—let everything be as she wishes. Nothing can save her, but perfect quiet and repose may prolong her existence."

The last week of September the wedding was to take place; and all was bustle and haste at Jocyln Hall. Mr. Legard was to stay for the wedding, at the express desire of Lady Thetford herself. She had seen him but very rarely since that first day, illness had compelled her to keep her room; but her interest in him was unabated, and she had sent for him to her apartment, and invited him to remain. And Mr. Legard, a good deal surprised, and a little flattered, consented at once.

"Very kind of Lady Thetford, you know, Miss Everard," Mr. Legard said, sauntering into the room where she sat with her ex-governess—Mr. Legard and Miss Everard were growing highly confidential of late—"to take such an interest in an utter stranger as she does in me."

May stole a glance from under her eyelashes at Mrs. Weymore; that lady sat nervous and scared-looking, and altogether uncomfortable, as she had a habit of doing in the young artist's presence.

"Very," Miss Everard said, dryly. "You ought to feel highly complimented, Mr. Legard, for it's a sort of kindness her ladyship is extremely chary of to utter strangers. Rather odd, isn't it, Mrs. Weymore?"

Mrs. Weymore's reply was a distressed, beseeching look. Mr. Legard saw it, and opened very wide his handsome, Saxon eyes.

"Eh?" he said, "it doesn't mean anything, does it? Mrs. Weymore looks mysterious, and I'm so stupid about these things. Lady Thetford doesn't know anything about me, does she?"

"Not that I know of," May said, with significant emphasis on the personal pronoun.

"Then Mrs. Weymore does! By Jove! I always thought Mrs. Weymore had an odd way of looking at me! And now, what is it?"

He turned his fair, resolute face to that lady with a smile hard to resist.

"I don't make much of a howling about my affairs, you know, Mrs. Weymore," he said; "but for all that, I am none the less interested in myself and my history. If you can open the mysteries a little you will be conferring a favor on me I can never repay. And I am positive from your look you can."

Mrs. Weymore turned away, and covered her face with a sort of sob. The young lady and gentleman exchanged startled glances.

"You can then?" Mr. Legard said, gravely, but growing very pale. "You know who I am?"

To his boundless consternation Mrs. Weymore rose up and fell at his feet, seizing his hands and covering them with kisses.

"I do! I do! I know who you are, and so shall you before this wedding takes place. But before I tell you I must speak to Lady Thetford."

Mr. Legard raised her up, his face as colorless as her own.

"To Lady Thetford! What has Lady Thetford to do with me?"

"Everything! She knows who you are as well as I do. I must speak to her first."

"Answer me one thing—is my name Vyking?"

"No. Pray, pray don't ask me any more questions. As soon as her ladyship is a little stronger, I will go to her and obtain her permission to speak. Keep what I have said a secret from Sir Rupert, and wait until then."

She rose up to go, so haggard and deploring-looking, that neither strove to detain her. The young man stared blankly after her as she left the room.

"At last!" he said, drawing a deep breath, "at last I shall know!"

There was a pause; then May spoke in a fluttering little voice.

"How very strange that Mrs. Weymore should know, of all persons in the world."

"Who is Mrs. Weymore? How long has she been here? Tell me all you know of her, Miss Everard."

"And that 'all' will be almost nothing. She came down from London as a nursery-governess to Rupert and me, a week or two after my arrival here, selected by the rector of St. Gosport. She was then what you see her now, a pale, subdued creature in widow's weeds, with the look of one who had seen trouble. I have known her so long, and always as such a white, still shadow, I suppose that is why it seems so odd."

Mrs. Weymore kept altogether out of Mr. Legard's way for the next week or two. She avoided May also, as much as possible, and shrunk so palpably from any allusion to the past scene, that May good naturedly bided her time in silence, though almost as impatient as Mr. Legard himself.

And whilst they waited the bridal eve came round, and Lady Thetford was much better, not able to quit her room, but strong enough to lie on a sofa and talk to her son and Col. Jocyln, with a flush on her cheek and sparkle in her eye—all unusual there.

The marriage was to take place in the village church; and there was to follow a grand ceremonial of a wedding-breakfast; and then the happy pair were to start at once on their bridal-tour.

"And I hope to see my boy return," Lady Thetford said, kissing him fondly. "I can hardly ask for more than that."

Late in the afternoon of that eventful wedding-eve, the ex-governess sought out Guy Legard, for the first time of her own accord. She found him in the young baronet's studio, with May, putting the finishing touches to that young lady's portrait. He started up at sight of his visitor, vividly interested. Mrs. Weymore was paler even than usual, but with a look of deep, quiet determination on her face no one had ever seen there before.

"You have come to keep your promise," the young man cried—"to tell me who I am?"

"I have come to keep my promise," Mrs. Weymore answered; "but I must speak to my lady first. I wanted to tell you that, before you sleep to-night, you shall know."

She left the studio, and the two sat there, breathless, expectant. Sir Rupert was dining at Jocyln Hall, Lady Thetford was alone in high spirits, and Mrs. Weymore was admitted at once.

"I wonder how long you must wait?" said May Everard.

"Heaven knows! Not long, I hope, or I shall go mad with impatience."

An hour passed—two—three, and still Mrs. Weymore was closeted with my lady, and still the pair in the studio waited.

CHAPTER XII.

MRS. WEYMORE'S STORY.

Lady Thetford sat up among her pillows and looked at her hired dependent with wide open eyes of astonishment. The pale, timid face of Mrs. Weymore wore a look altogether new.

"Listen to your story! My dear Mrs. Weymore, what possible interest can your story have for me?"

"More than you think, my lady. You are so much stronger to-day than usual, and Sir Rupert's marriage is so very near that I must speak now or never."

"Sir Rupert!" my lady gasped. "What has your story to do with Sir Rupert?"

"You will hear," Mrs. Weymore said, very sadly. "Heaven knows I should have told you long ago; but it is a story few would care to tell. A cruel and shameful story of wrong and misery; for, my lady, I have been cruelly wronged by one who was once very near to you."

Lady Thetford turned ashen white.

"Very near to me! Do you mean——"

"My lady, listen, and you shall hear. All those years that I have been with you, I have not been what I seemed. My name is not Weymore. My name is Thetford—as yours is."

An awful terror had settled down on my lady's face. Her lips moved, but she did not speak. Her eyes were fixed on the sad, set face before her, with a wild, expectant stare.

"I was a widow when I came to you," Mrs. Weymore went on to say, "but long before I had known that worst widowhood, desertion. I ran away from my happy home, from the kindest father and mother that ever lived; I ran away and was married and deserted before I was eighteen years old.

"He came to our village, a remote place, my lady, with a local celebrity for its trout streams, and for nothing else. He came, the man whom I married, on a visit to the great house of the place. We had not the remotest connection with the house, or I might have known his real name. When I did know him it was as Mr. Noel—he told me himself, and I never thought of doubting it. I was as simple and confiding as it is possible for the simplest village girl to be, and all the handsome stranger told me was gospel truth; and my life only began, I thought, from the hour I saw him first.

"I met him at the trout streams fishing, and alone. I had come to while the long, lazy hours under the trees. He spoke to me—the handsome stranger, whom I had seen riding through the village beside the squire, like a young prince; and I was only too pleased and flattered by his notice. It is many years ago, my lady, and Mr. Noel took a fancy to my pink-and-white face and fair curls, as fine gentlemen will. It was only fancy—never, at its best, love; or he would not have deserted me pitilessly as he did. I know it now; but then I took the tinsel for pure gold, and would as soon have doubted the Scripture as his lightest word.

"My lady, it is a very old story, and very often told. We met by stealth and in secret; and weeks passed and I never learned he was other than what I knew him. I loved with my whole foolish, trusting heart, strongly and selfishly; and I was ready to give up home, and friends and parents—all the world for him. All the world, but not my good name, and he knew that; and, my lady, we were married—really and truly and honestly married, in a little church in Berkshire, in Windsor; and the marriage is recorded in the register of the church, and I have the marriage certificate here in my possession."

Mrs. Weymore touched her bosom as she spoke, and looked with earnest, truthful eyes at Lady Thetford. But Lady Thetford's face was averted and not to be seen.

"His fancy for me was as fleeting as all his fancies; but it was strong enough and reckless enough whilst it lasted to make him forget all consequences. For it was surely a reckless act for a gentleman, such as he was, to marry the daughter of a village schoolmaster.

"There was but one witness to our marriage—my husband's servant— George Vyking. I never liked the man; he was crafty, and cunning, and treacherous, and ready for any deed of evil; but he was in his master's confidence, and took a house for us at Windsor and lived with us, and kept his master's secrets well."

Mrs. Weymore paused, her hands fluttering in painful unrest. The averted face of Lady Thetford never turned, but a smothered voice bade her go on.

"A year passed, my lady, and I still lived in the house at Windsor, but quite alone now. My punishment had begun very early; two or three months sufficed to weary my husband of his childish village girl, and make him thoroughly repent his folly. I saw it from the first—he never tried to hide it from me; his absence grew longer and longer, more and more frequent, until at last he ceased coming altogether. Vyking, the valet, came and went;

and Vyking told me the truth—the hard, cruel, bitter truth, that I was never to see my husband more.

"'It was the maddest act of a mad young man's life,' Vyking said to me, coolly, 'and he's repented of it, as I knew he would repent. You'll never see him again, mistress, and you needn't search for him, either. When you find last winter's snow, last autumn's partridges, then you may hope to find him.'

"'But I am his wife,' I said; 'nothing can undo that—his lawful, wedded wife.'

"'Yes,' said Vyking, 'his wife fast enough; but there's the law of divorce, and there's no witness but me alive, and you can do your best; and the best you can do is to take it easy and submit. He'll provide for you handsomely; and when he gets the divorce, if you like, I'll marry you myself.'

"I had grown to expect some such revelation, I had been neglected so long. My lady, I don't speak of my feelings, my anguish and shame, and remorse and despair—I only tell you here simple facts. But in the days and weeks which followed, I suffered as I never can suffer again in this world.

"I was held little better than a prisoner in the house at Windsor after that; and I think Vyking never gave up the hope that I would one day consent to marry him. More than once I tried to run away, to get on the track of my betrayer, but always to be met and foiled. I have gone down on my knees to that man Vyking, but I might as well have knelt to a statue of stone.

"'I'll tell you what we'll do,' he said, 'we'll go to London. People are beginning to look and talk about here; there they know how to mind their own business.'

"I consented readily enough. My one hope now was to find the man who had wronged me, and in London I thought I stood a better chance that at Windsor. We started, Vyking and I; but driving to the station we met with an accident, our horse ran away and I was thrown out; after that I hardly remember anything for a long time.

"Weeks passed before I recovered. Then I was told my baby had been born and died. I listened in a sort of dull apathy; I had suffered so much that the sense of suffering was dulled and blunted. I knew Vyking well enough not to trust him or believe him; but I was powerless to act, and could only turn my face to the wall and pray to die.

"But I grew strong, and Vyking took me to London, and left me in respectably-furnished lodgings. I might have escaped easily enough here, but the energy even to wish for freedom was gone; I sat all day long in a state of miserable, listless languor, heart-weary, heart-sick, worn out.

"One day Vyking came to my rooms in a furious state of passion. He and his master had quarreled. I never knew about what; and Vyking had been ignominiously dismissed. The valet tore up and down my parlor in a towering passion.

"'I'll make Sir Noel pay for it, or my name's not Vyking,' he cried. 'He thinks because he's married an heiress he can defy me now. But there's a law in this land to punish bigamy; and I'll have him up for bigamy the moment he's back from his wedding tour.'

"I turned and looked at him, but very quietly, 'Sir Noel,' I said. 'Do you mean my husband?'

"'I mean Miss Vandeleur's husband now,' said Vyking. '*You'll* never see him again, my girl. Yes, he's Sir Noel Thetford, of Thetford Towers, Devonshire; and you can go and call on his pretty new wife as soon as she comes home.'

"I turned away and looked out of the window without a word. Vyking looked at me curiously.

"'Oh! we've got over it, have we; and we're going to take it easy and not make a scene? Now that's what I call sensible. And you'll come forward and swear Sir Noel guilty of bigamy?'

"'No,' I said, 'I never will.'

"'You won't—and why not?'

"'Never mind why. I don't think you would understand if I told you—only I won't.'

"'Couldn't you be coaxed?'

"'No.'

"'Don't be too sure. Perhaps I could tell you something that might move you, quiet as you are. What if I told you your baby did not die that time, but was alive and well?'

"I knew a scene was worse than useless with this man, tears and entreaties thrown away. I heard his last words and started to my feet with outstretched hands.

"'Vyking, for the dear Lord's sake, have pity on a desolate woman, and tell me the truth.'

"'I am telling you the truth. Your boy is alive and well, and I've christened him Guy—Guy Vyking. Don't you be scared—he's all safe; and the day you appear in court against Sir Noel, that day he shall be restored to you. Now don't you go and get excited, think it over, and let me know your decision when I come back.'

"He left the room before I could answer, and I never saw Vyking again. The next day, reading the morning paper, I saw the arrest of a pair of house-breakers, and the name of the chief was George Vyking, late valet to Sir Noel Thetford. I tried to get to see him in prison, but failed. His trial came on, his sentence was transportation for ten years; and Vyking left England, carrying my secret with him.

"I had something left to live for now—the thought of my child. But where was I to find him, where to look? I, who had not a penny in the wide world. If I had had the means, I would have come to Devonshire to seek out the man who had so basely wronged me; but as I was, I could as soon have gone to the antipodes. Oh! it was a bitter, bitter time, that long, hard struggle, with starvation—a time it chills my blood even now to look back upon.

"I was still in London, battling with grim poverty, when, six months later, I read in the *Times* the awfully sudden death of Sir Noel Thetford, Baronet.

"My lady, I am not speaking of the effect of that blow—I dare not to you, as deeply wronged as myself. You were with him in his dying moments, and surely he told you the truth then; surely he acknowledged the great wrong he had done you?"

Mrs. Weymore paused, and Lady Thetford turned her face, her ghastly, white face, for the first time, to answer.

"He did—he told me all; I know your story to be true."

"Thank God! Oh, thank God! And he acknowledged his first marriage?"

"Yes; the wrong he did you was venial to that which he did me—I, who never was his wife, never for one poor moment had a right to his name."

Mrs. Weymore sunk down on her knees by the couch, and passionately kissed the lady's hand.

"My lady! my lady! And you will forgive me for coming here? I did not know, when I answered Mr. Knight's advertisement, where I was coming; and when I did, I could not resist the temptation of looking on his son. Oh, my lady! you will forgive me, and bear witness to the truth of my story."

"I will; I always meant to before I died. And that young man—that Guy Legard—you know he is your son?"

"I knew it from the first. My lady, you will let me tell him at once, will you not? And Sir Rupert? Oh, my lady! he ought to know."

Lady Thetford covered her face with a groan.

"I promised his father on his death-bed to tell him long ago, to seek for his rightful heir—and see how I have kept my word. But I could not—I could not! It was not in human nature—not in such a nature as mine, wronged as I have been."

"But now—oh, my dear lady! now you will?"

"Yes, now, on the verge of the grave, I may surely speak. I dare not die with my promise unkept. This very night," Lady Thetford cried, sitting up, flushed and excited, "my boy shall know all—he shall not marry in ignorance of whom he really is. Aileen has the fortune of a princess; and Aileen will not love him less for the title he must lose. When he comes home, Mrs. Weymore, send him to me, and send your son with him, and I will tell them all."

CHAPTER XIII.

"THERE IS MANY A SLIP."

A room that was like a picture—a carpet of rose-buds gleaming through rich green moss, lounges piled with downy-silk pillows, a bed curtained in foamy lace, a pretty room—Aileen Jocyln's *chambre-a-coucher*, and looking like a picture herself, in a flowing morning-robe, the rich, dark hair falling heavy and unbound to her waist, Aileen Jocyln lay among piles of scarlet cushions, like some young Eastern Sultana.

Lay and music with, oh! such an infinitely happy smile upon her exquisite face; mused, as happy youth, loving and beloved, upon its bridal-eve doth muse. Nay, on her bridal-day, for the dainty little French clock on the bracket was pointing its golden hands to three.

The house was very still; all had retired late, busy with preparations for the morrow, and Miss Jocyln had but just dismissed her maid. Every one, probably, but herself, was asleep; and she, in her unutterable bliss, was too happy for slumber. She arose presently, walked to the window and looked out. The late setting moon still swung in the sky; the stars still spangled the cloudless blue, and shone serene on the purple bosom of the far-spreading sea; but in the east the first pale glimmer of the new day shone—her happy wedding day. The girl slid down on her knees, her hands clasped, her radiant face glorified with love and bliss, turned ecstatically, as some faithful follower of the prophet might, to that rising glory of the east.

"Oh!" Aileen thought, gazing around over the dark, deep sea, the star-gemmed sky, and the green radiance and sweetness of the earth, "what a beautiful, blissful world it is, and I the happiest creature in it!"

Kneeling there, with her face still turned to that luminous East, the blissful bride fell asleep; slept, and dreamed dreams as joyful as her waking thoughts, and no shadow of that sweeping cloud that was to blacken all her world so soon fell upon her.

Hours passed, and still Aileen slept. Then came an imperative knock at her door—again and again, louder each time; and then Aileen started up, fully awake. Her room was flooded with sunshine, and countless birds sang their glorias in the swaying green gloom of the branches, and the ceaseless sea was all a-glitter with sparkling sun-light.

"Come in," Miss Jocyln said. It was her maid, she thought—and she walked over to an arm-chair and composedly sat down.

The door opened, and Col. Jocyln, not Fanchon, appeared, an open note in his hand, his face full of trouble.

"Papa!" Aileen cried, starting up in alarm.

"Bad news, my daughter—very bad! very sorrowful! Read that."

The note was very brief, in a spidery, female hand.

> "DEAR COL. JOCYLN:—We are in the greatest trouble. Poor Lady Thetford died with awful suddenness this morning in one of those dreadful spasms. We are all nearly distracted. Rupert bears it better than any of us. Pray come over as soon as you can.
>
> "MAY. EVERARD."

Aileen Jocyln sunk back in her seat, pale and trembling.

"Dead! Oh, papa! papa!"

"It is very sad, my dear, and very shocking and terribly unfortunate that it should have occurred just at this time. A postponed wedding is ever ominous of evil."

"Oh! pray, papa, don't think of that! Don't think of me! Poor Lady Thetford! Poor Rupert! You will go over at once, papa, will you not?"

"Certainly, my dear. And I will tell the servants, so that when our guests arrive you may not be disturbed. Since it was to be," muttered the Indian officer under his moustache. "I would give half my fortune that it had been one day later. A postponed marriage is the most ominous thing under the sun."

He left the room, and Aileen sat with her hands clasped, and an unutterable awe overpowering every other feeling. She forgot her own disappointment in the awful mystery of sudden death. Her share of the trial was light—a year of waiting, more or less; what did it matter, since Rupert loved her unchangeably? but, poor Lady Aileen, remembering how much the dead woman had loved her, and how fondly she had welcomed her as a daughter, covered her face with her hands, and wept as she might have wept for her own mother.

"I never knew a mother's love or care," Aileen thought; "and I was doubly happy in knowing I was to have one at last. And now—and now——"

It was a drearily long morning to the poor bride elect, sitting alone in her chamber. She heard the roll of carriages up the drive, the pause that ensued, and then their departure. She wondered how *he* bore it best of all, May had said; but, then, he was ever still and strong and self-restrained. She knew how dear that poor, ailing mother had ever been to him, and she knew how bitterly he would feel her loss.

"They talk of presentiments," mused Miss Jocyln, walking wearily to and fro; "and see how happy and hopeful I was this morning, whilst she lay dead and he mourned. If I only dared go to him—my own Rupert!"

It was late in the afternoon before Col. Jocyln returned. He strode straight to his daughter's presence, wearing a pale, fagged face.

"Well, papa?" she asked, faintly.

"My pale Aileen!" he said, kissing her fondly; "my poor, patient girl! I am sorry you must undergo this trial, and," knitting his brows, "such talk as it will make."

"Don't think of me, papa—my share is surely the lightest. But Rupert—" wistfully faltering.

"There's something odd about Rupert; he was very fond of his mother, and he takes this a great deal too quietly. He looks like a man slowly turning to stone, with a face white and stern; and he never asked for you. He sat there with folded arms and that petrified face, gazing on his dead, until it chilled my blood to look at him. There's something odd and unnatural in this frozen calm. And, oh! by-the-bye! I forgot to tell you the strangest thing— May Everard it was told me; that painter fellow—what's his name—"

"Legard, papa?"

"Yes, Legard. He turns out to be the son of Mrs. Weymore; they discovered it last night. He was there in the room, with the most dazed and mystified and altogether bewildered expression of countenance I ever saw a man wear, and May and Mrs. Weymore sat crying incessantly. I couldn't see what occasion there was for the governess and the painter there in that room of death, and I said so to Miss Everard. There's something mysterious in the matter, for her face flushed and she stammered something about startling family secrets that had come to light, and the over-excitement of which had hastened Lady Thetford's end. I don't like the look of things, and I'm altogether in the dark. That painter resembles the Thetford's a great deal too closely for the mere work of chance; and yet, if Mrs. Weymore is his mother, I don't see how there can be anything in *that*. It's odd—confoundedly odd!"

Col. Jocyln rumbled on as he walked the floor, his brows knitted into a swarthy frown. His daughter sat and eyed him wistfully.

"Did no one ask for me, papa? Am I not to go over?"

"Sir Rupert didn't ask for you! May Everard did, and I promised to fetch you to-morrow. Aileen, things at Thetford Towers have a suspicious look to-day; I can't see the light yet, but I suspect something wrong. It may be the very best thing that could possibly happen, this postponed marriage; I shall make Sir Rupert clear matters up completely before my daughter becomes his wife."

Col. Jocyln, according to promise, took his daughter to Thetford Towers next morning. With bated breath and beating heart and noiseless tread, Aileen Jocyln entered the house of mourning, which yesterday she had thought to enter a bride. Dark and still, and desolate it lay, the morning light shut out, unbroken silence everywhere.

"And this is the end of earth, its glory and its bliss," Aileen thought as she followed her father slowly up-stairs, "the solemn wonder of the winding-sheet and the grave."

There were two watchers in the dark room when they entered—May Everard, pale and quiet, and the young artist, Guy Legard. Even in that moment, Col. Jocyln could not repress a supercilious stare of wonder to behold the housekeeper's son in the death-chamber of Lady Thetford. And yet it seemed strangely his place, for it might have been one of those lusty old Thetfords, framed and glazed up-stairs, stepped out of the canvas and dressed in the fashion of the day.

"Very bad tastes all the same," the proud old colonel thought, with a frown: "very bad taste on the part of Sir Rupert. I shall speak to him on the subject presently."

He stood in silence beside his daughter, looking down at the marble face. May, shivering drearily in a large shawl, and looking like a wan little spirit, was speaking in whispers to Aileen.

"We persuaded Rupert—Mr. Legard and I—to go and lie down; he has neither eaten nor slept since his mother died. Oh, Aileen! I am so sorry for you!"

"Hush!" raising one tremulous hand and turning away; "she was as dear to me as my own mother could have been! Don't think of me."

"Shall we not see Sir Rupert?" the colonel asked. "I should like to, particularly."

"I think not—unless you remain for some hours. He is completely worn out, poor fellow!"

"How comes that young man here, Miss Everard?" nodding in the direction of Mr. Legard, who had withdrawn to a remote corner. "He may be a very especial friend of Sir Rupert's—but don't you think he presumes on that friendship?"

Miss Everard's eyes flashed angrily.

"No, sir! I think nothing of the sort! Mr. Legard has a perfect right to be in this room, or any other room at Thetford Towers. It is by Rupert's particular request he remains!"

The colonel frowned again, and turned his back upon the speaker.

"Aileen," he said, haughtily, "as Sir Rupert is not visible, nor likely to be for some time, perhaps you had better not linger. To-morrow, after the funeral, I shall speak to him very seriously."

Miss Jocyln arose. She would rather have lingered, but she saw her father's annoyed face and obeyed him immediately. She bent and kissed the cold, white face, awful with the dread majesty of death.

"For the last time, my friend, my mother," she murmured, "until we meet in heaven."

She drew her veil over her face to hide her falling tears, and silently followed the stern and displeased Indian officer down-stairs and out of the house. She looked back wistfully once at the gray, old ivy-grown facade; but who was to tell her of the weary, weary months and years that would pass before she crossed that stately threshold again?

It was a very grand and imposing ceremonial, that burial of Lady Thetford; and side by side with the heir walked the unknown painter, Guy Legard. Col. Jocyln was not the only friend of the family shocked on this occasion. What could Sir Rupert mean? And what did Mr. Legard mean by looking ten times more like the old Thetford race than Sir Noel's own son and heir?

It was a miserable day, this day of the funeral. There was a sky of lead hanging low like a pall, and it was almost dark in the rainy afternoon gloaming when Col. Jocyln and Sir Rupert Thetford stood alone before the village church. Lady Thetford slept with the rest of the name in the stony vaults; the fair-haired artist stood in the porch, and Sir Rupert, with a face wan and stern, and spectral, in the dying daylight, stood face to face with the colonel.

"A private interview," the colonel was repeating; "most certainly, Sir Rupert. Will you come with me to Jocyln Hall? My daughter will wish to see you."

The young man nodded, went back a moment to speak to Legard, and then followed the colonel into the carriage. The drive was a very silent one—a vague, chilling presentiment of impending evil on the Indian officer as he uneasily watched the young man who had so nearly been his son.

Aileen Jocyln, roaming like a restless ghost through the lonely, lofty rooms, saw them alight, and came out to the hall to meet her betrothed. She held out both hands shyly, looking up, half in fear, in the rigid, death-white face of her lover.

"Aileen!"

He took the hands and held them fast a moment; then dropped them and turned to the colonel.

"Now, Col. Jocyln."

The colonel led the way into the library. Sir Rupert paused a moment on the threshold to answer Aileen's pleading glance.

"Only for a few moments, Aileen," he said, his eyes softening with infinite love; "in half an hour my fate shall be decided. Let that fate be what it may, I shall be true to you while life lasts."

With these enigmatical words, he followed the colonel into the library, and the polished oaken door closed between him and Aileen.

CHAPTER XIV.

PARTED.

Half an hour had passed.

Up and down the long drawing-room Aileen wandered aimlessly, oppressed with a dread of she knew not what, a prescience of evil, vague as it was terrible. The dark gloom of the rainy evening was not darker than that brooding shadow in her deep, dusky eyes.

In the library Col. Jocyln stood facing his son-in-law elect, staring like a man bereft of his senses. The melancholy, half light coming through the oriel window by which he stood, fell full upon the face of Rupert Thetford, white and cold, and set as marble.

"My God!" the Indian officer said, with wild eyes of terror and affright, "what is this you are telling me?"

"The truth, Col. Jocyln—the simple truth. Would to Heaven I had known it years ago—this shameful story of wrong-doing and misery!"

"I don't comprehend—I can't comprehend this impossible tale, Sir Rupert."

"That is a misnomer now, Col. Jocyln. I am no longer *Sir* Rupert."

"Do you mean to say you credit this wild story of a former marriage of Sir Noel's? Do you really believe your late governess to have been your father's wife?"

"I believe it, colonel. I have facts and statements and dying words to prove it. On my father's death-bed he made my mother swear to tell the truth; to repair the wrong he had done; to seek out his son, concealed by his valet, Vyking, and restore him to his rights! My mother never, kept that promise—the cruel wrong done to herself was too bitter; and at my birth she resolved never to keep it. I should not atone for the sin of my father; his elder son should never deprive *her* child of his birthright. My poor mother! You know the cause of that mysterious trouble which fell upon her at my father's death, and which darkened her life to the last. Shame, remorse, anger—shame for herself—a wife only in name; remorse for her broken vow to the dead, and anger against that erring dead man."

"But you told me she had hunted him up and provided for him," said the mystified colonel.

"Yes; she saw an advertisement in a London paper calling upon Vyking to take charge of the boy he had left twelve years before. Now, Vyking, the valet, had been transported for house-breaking long before that, and my mother answered the advertisement. There could be no doubt the child was the child Vyking had taken charge of—Sir Noel Thetford's rightful heir. My mother left him with the painter, Legard, with whom he had grew up, whose name he took, and he is now at Thetford Towers."

"I thought the likeness meant something," muttered the colonel; "his paternity is plainly enough written in his face. And so," raising his voice, "Mrs. Weymore recognized her son. Really, your story runs like a melodrama, where the hero turns out to be a duke and his mother knows the strawberry mark on his arm. Well, sir, if Mrs. Weymore is Sir Noel's rightful widow, and Guy Legard his rightful son and heir—pray what are you?"

The colorless face of the young man turned dark-red for an instant, then whiter than before.

"My, mother was as truly and really Sir Noel's wife as women can be the wife of man in the sight of Heaven. The crime was his; the shame and suffering hers; the atonement mine. Sir Noel's elder son shall be Sir Noel's heir—I will play usurper no longer. To-morrow I leave St. Gosport; the day after, England—never, perhaps, to return."

"You are mad," Col. Jocyln said, turning very pale; "you do not mean it."

"I am not mad, and I do mean it. I may be unfortunate; but, I pray God, never a villain! Right is right; my brother Guy is the rightful heir—not I!"

"And Aileen?" Col. Jocyln's face turned dark and rigid as iron as he spoke his daughter's name.

Rupert Thetford turned away his changing face, quite ghastly now.

"It shall be as she says. Aileen is too noble and just herself not to honor me for doing right."

"It shall be as I say," returned Col. Jocyln, with a voice that rang and an eye that flashed. "My daughter comes of a proud and stainless race, and never shall she mate with one less stainless. Hear me out, young man. It won't do to fire up—plain words are best suited to a plain case. All that has passed betwixt you and Miss Jocyln must be as if it had never been. The heir of Thetford Towers, honorably born, I consented she should marry; but, dearly as I love her, I would see her dead at my feet before she should mate with one who was nameless and impoverished. You said just now the atonement was yours—you said right; go, and never return."

- 83 -

He pointed to the door; the young man, stonily still, took his hat.

"Will you not permit your daughter, Col. Jocyln, to speak for herself?" he said, at the door.

"No, sir. I know my daughter—my proud, high-spirited Aileen—and my answer is hers. I wish you good-night."

He swung round abruptly, turning his back upon his visitor. Rupert Thetford, without one word, turned and walked out of the house.

The bewildering rapidity of the shocks he had received had stunned him— he could not feel the pain now. There was a dull sense of aching torture over him from head to foot—but the acute edge was dulled; he walked along through the black night like a man drugged and stupefied. He was only conscious intensely of one thing—a wish to get away, never to set foot in St. Gosport again.

Like one walking in his sleep, he reached Thetford Towers, his old home, every tree and stone of which was dear to him. He entered at once, passed into the drawing-room, and found Guy, the artist, sitting before the fire staring blankly into the coals, and May Everard roaming restlessly up and down, the firelight falling dully on her black robes and pale, tear-stained face. Both started at his entrance—all wet, and wild, and haggard; but neither spoke. There was that in his face which froze the words on their lips.

"I am going away to-morrow," he said, abruptly, leaning against the mantle, and looking at them with weird, spectral eyes.

May uttered a faint cry; Guy faced him almost fiercely.

"Going away! What do you mean, Sir Rupert? We are going away together, if you like."

"No; I go alone. You remain here; it is your place now."

"Never!" cried the young artist—"never! I will go out and die like a dog, in a ditch, before I rob you of your birthright!"

"You reverse matters," said Rupert Thetford; "it is I who have robbed you, unwittingly, for too many years. I promised my mother on her death-bed, as she promised my father on his, that you should have your right, and I will keep that promise. Guy, dear old fellow! don't let us quarrel, now that we are brothers, after being friends so long. Take what is your own; the world is all before me, and surely I am man enough to win my own way. Not one other word; you shall not come with me; you might as well talk to these stone walls and try to move them as to me. To-morrow I go, and go alone."

"Alone!" It was May who breathlessly repeated the word.

"Alone! All the ties that bound me here are broken; I go alone and single-handed to fight the battle of life. Guy, I have spoken to the rector about you—you will find him your friend and aider; and May is to make her home at the rectory. And now," turning suddenly and moving to the door, "as I start early to-morrow, I believe I'll retire early. Good-night."

And then he was gone, and Guy and May were left staring at each other with blank faces.

The storm of wind and rain sobbed itself out before midnight, and in the bluest of skies, heralded by banners of rosy clouds, rose up the sun next morning. Before that rising sun had gilded the tops of the tallest oaks in the park he, who had so lately called it all his own, had opened the heavy oaken door and passed from Thetford Towers, as home, forever. The house was very still—no one had risen; he had left a note to Guy, with a few brief, warm words of farewell.

"Better so," he thought—"better so! He and May will be happy together, for I know he loves her and she him. The memory of my leave-taking shall never come to cloud their united lives."

One last backward glance at the eastern windows turning to gold; at the sea blushing back the first glance of the day-king; at the waving trees and swelling meadows, and then he had passed down the avenue, out through the massive entrance-gates, and was gone.

CHAPTER XV.

AFTER FIVE YEARS.

Moonlight falling like a silvery veil over Venice—a crystal clear crescent in a purple sky shimmering on palace and prison, churches, squares and canals, on the gliding gondolas and the flitting forms passing like noiseless shadows to and fro.

A young lady leaned from a window of a vast Venetian hotel, gazing thoughtfully at the silver-lighted landscape, so strange, so unreal, so dream-like to her unaccustomed eyes. A young lady, stately and tall, with a pale, proud face, and a statuesque sort of beauty that was perfect in its way. She was dressed in trailing robes of crape and bombazine, and the face, turned to the moonlight, was cold and still as marble.

She turned her eyes from the moonlit canal, down which dark gondolas floated to the music of the gay gondolier's song; once, as an English voice in the piazza below sung a stave of a jingling barcarole—

"Oh! gay we row where full tides flow!And bear our bounding pinnace;And leap along where song meets song,Across the waves of Venice."

The singer, a tall young man, with a florid face and yellow side-whiskers, an unmistakable son of the "right little, tight little" island, paused in his song, as another man, stepping through an open window, struck him an airy, sledge-hammer slap on the back.

"I ought to know that voice," said the last comer.

"Mortimer, my lad, how goes it?"

"Stafford!" cried the singer, seizing the outstretched hand in a genuine English grip, "happy to meet you, old boy, in the land of romance! La Fabre told me you were coming, but who would look for you so soon! I thought you were doing Sorrento?"

"Got tired of Sorrento," said Stafford, taking his arm for a walk up and down the piazza; "there's a fever there, too—quite an epidemic—malignant typhus. Discretion is the better part of valor where Sorrento fevers are concerned. I left."

"When did you reach Venice?" asked Mortimer, lighting a cigar.

"An hour ago; and now who's here? Any one I know!"

"Lots. The Cholmonadeys, the Lythons, the Howards, of Leighwood; and, by-the-bye, they have with them the Marble Bride."

"The which?" asked Mr. Stafford.

"The Marble Bride, the Princess Frostina; otherwise Miss Aileen Jocyln, of Jocyln Hall Devonshire. You knew the old colonel, I think; he died over a year ago, you remember."

"Ah, yes! I remember. Is she here with the Howards, and as handsome as ever, no doubt?"

"Handsome, to my mind, with an uplifted and unapproachable sort of beauty. A fellow might as soon love some bright particular star, etc., as the fabulously wealthy heiress of all the Jocylns. She has no end of suitors—all the best men here bow at the shrine of the ice-cold Aileen, and all in vain."

"You among the rest, my friend?" with a light laugh.

"No, by Jove!" cried Mr. Mortimer; "that sort of thing—the marble style, you know—never was to my taste. I admire Miss Jocyln immensely—just as I do the moon up there, with no particular desire ever to be nearer."

"What was that story I heard once, five years ago, about a broken engagement? Wasn't Thetford of that ilk the hero of the tale?—the romantic Thetford, who resigned his title and estate to a mysteriously-found elder brother, you know. The story ran through the papers and the clubs at the time like wildfire, and set the whole country talking, I remember. She was engaged to him, wasn't she, and broke off?"

"So goes the story—but who knows? I recollect that odd affair perfectly well; it was like the melodramas on the sunny side of the Thames. I know the 'mysteriously-found elder brother,' too—very fine fellow, Sir Guy Thetford, and married to the prettiest little wife the sun shines on. I must say Rupert Thetford behaved wonderfully well in that unpleasant business; very few men would do as he did—they would, at least, have made a fight for the title and estates. By-the-way, I wonder whatever became of him?"

"I left him at Sorrento," said Stafford, coolly.

"The deuce you did! What was he doing there?"

"Raving in the fever; so the people told me with whom he stopped. I just discovered he was in the place as I was about to leave it. He had fallen very low, I fancy; his pictures didn't sell, I suppose; he has been in the painting line since he ceased to be Sir Rupert, and the world has gone against him. Rather hard on him to lose fortune, title, home, bride, and all at one fell swoop. Some women there are who would go with their plighted husbands to beggary; but I suppose the lovely Aileen is not one of them."

"And so you left him ill of the fever? Poor fellow!"

"Dangerously ill."

"And the people with whom he is will take very little care of him; he's as good as dead. Let us go in—I want to have a look at the latest English papers."

The two men passed in, out of the moonlight, off the piazza, all unconscious that they had had a listener. The pale watcher in the trailing black robes, scarcely heeding them at first, had grown more and more absorbed in the careless conversation. She caught her breath in quick, short gasps, the dark eyes dilated, the slender hands pressed themselves tight over the throbbing heart. As they went in off the balcony she slid from her seat and held up her clasped hands to the luminous night sky.

"Hear me, oh, God!" the white lips cried—"I, who have aided in wrecking a noble heart—hear me, and help me to keep my vow! I offer my whole life in atonement for the cruel and wicked past. If he dies, I shall go to my grave his unwedded widow. If he lives——"

Her voice faltered and died out, her face drooped forward on the window-sill, and the flashing moonlight fell like a benediction on the bowed young head.

CHAPTER XVI.

AT SORRENTO.

The low light in the western sky was dying out; the bay of Naples lay rosy in the haze of the dying day; and on this scene an invalid, looking from a window high up on the sea-washed cliff at Sorrento, gazed languidly.

For he was surely an invalid who sat in that window chair and gazed at the wondrous Italian sea and that lovely Italian sky; surely an invalid, with that pallid face, those spectral, hollow eyes, those sunken cheeks, those bloodless lips; surely an invalid, and one but lately risen from the very gates of death—a pale shadow, worn and weak as a child.

As he sits there, where he has sat for hours, lonely and alone, the door opens, and an English face looks in—the face of an Englishman of the lower classes.

"A visitor for you, sir—just come, and a-foot; a lady, sir. She will not give her name, but wishes to see you most particular, if you please."

"A lady! To see me?"

The invalid opens his great, dark eyes in wonder as he speaks.

"Yes, sir; an English lady, sir, dressed in black, and a wearing of a thick veil. She asked for Mr. Rupert Thetford as soon as she see me, as plain, as plain, sir——"

The young man in the chair started, half rose, and then sank back—a wild, eager light lit in the hollow eyes.

"Let her come in; I will see her!"

The man disappeared; there was an instant's pause, then a tall, slender figure, draped and veiled in black, entered alone.

The visitor stood still. Once more the invalid attempted to rise, once more his strength failed him. The lady threw back her veil with a sudden motion.

"My God, Aileen!"

"Rupert!"

She was on her knees before him, lifting her suppliant hands.

"Forgive me! Forgive me! I have seemed the most heartless and cruel of women! But I, too, have suffered. I am base and unworthy; but, oh! forgive me, if you can!"

The old love, stronger than death, shone in her eyes, plead in her passionate, sobbing voice, and went to his very heart.

"I have been so wretched, so wretched all these miserable years! Whilst my father lived I would not disobey his stern command that I was never to attempt to see or hear from you, and at his death I could not. You seemed lost to me and the world. Only by the merest accident I heard in Venice you were here, and ill—dying. I lost no time, I came hither at once, hoping against hope to find you alive. Thank God I did come! Oh, Rupert! Rupert! for the sake of the past forgive me!"

"Forgive you!" and he tried to raise her. "Aileen—darling!"

His weak arms encircled her, and the pale lips pressed passionate kisses on the tear-wet face.

So, whilst the red glory of the sunset lay on the sea, and till the silver stars spangled the sky, the reunited lovers sat in the soft haze as Adam and Eve may have in the loveliness of Eden.

"How long since you left England?" Rupert asked at length.

"Two years ago; poor papa died in the south of France. You mustn't blame him too much, Rupert."

"My dearest, we will talk of blaming no one. And Guy and May are married? I knew they would be."

"Did you? I was so surprised when I read it in the *Times*; for you know May and I never corresponded—she was frantically angry with me. Do they know you are here?"

"No; I rarely write, and I am constantly moving about; but I know Guy is very much beloved in St. Gosport. We will go back to England one of these days, my darling, and give them the greatest surprise they have received since Sir Guy Thetford learned who he really was."

He smiled as he said it—the old bright smile she remembered so well. Tears of joy filled the beautiful, upturned eyes.

"And you will go back? Oh, Rupert! it needed but this to complete my happiness!"

He drew her closer, and then there was a long, delicious silence, whilst they watched together the late-rising moon climbing the misty hills above Castlemare.

CHAPTER XVII.

AT HOME.

Another sunset, red and gorgeous, over swelling English meadows, waving trees, and grassy terrace, lighting up with its crimson radiance the gray forest of Thetford Towers.

In the pretty, airy summer drawing-room, this red sunset streams through open western windows, kindling everything into living light. It falls on the bright-haired, girlish figure, dressed in floating white, seated in an arm-chair in the center of the room: too childish looking, you might fancy, at first sight, to be mamma to that fat baby she holds in her lap; but she is not a bit too childish. And that is papa, tall and handsome and happy, who leans over the chair and looks as men do look on what is the apple of their eye and the pride of their heart.

"It is high time baby was christened, Guy," Lady Thetford—for, of course, Lady Thetford it is—was saying; "and, do you know, I'm really at a loss for a name. You won't let me call him Guy, and I shan't call him Noel—and so what is it to be?"

"Rupert, of course," Sir Guy suggests; and little Lady Thetford pouts.

"He doesn't deserve the compliment. Shabby fellow! To keep wandering about the world as he does, and never to answer one's letter; and I sent him half a ream last time, if I sent him a sheet, telling all about baby, and asking him to come and be godfather, and coaxing him with the eloquence of a female Demos—what-you-may-call-him. And to think it should be all of no use! To think of not receiving a line in return! It is using me shamefully, and I don't believe I will call baby Rupert."

"Oh, yes you will, my dear! Well, Smithers, what is it?"

For Mr. Smithers, the butler, stood in the doorway, with a very pale and startled face.

"It's a gentleman—leastways a lady—leastways a lady and gentleman. Oh! here they come theirselves!"

Mr. Smithers retired precipitately, still pale and startled of visage, as a gentleman, with a lady on his arm, stood before Sir Guy and Lady Thetford.

There was a cry, a half shout, from the young baronet, a wild shriek from the lady. She sprung to her feet, and, nearly dropped the precious baby.

"Rupert! Aileen!"

She never got any further—this impetuous little Lady Thetford; for she was kissing first one, then the other, crying and laughing and talking, all in one breath.

"Oh, what a surprise this is! Oh, Rupert! I'm so glad, so glad to see you again! Oh, Aileen! I never, never hoped for this! Oh! good gracious, Guy, did you ever!"

But Guy was wringing his brother's hand, with bright tears standing in his eyes, and quite unable to reply.

"And this is the baby, May? The wonderful baby you wrote me so much about," Mr. Rupert Thetford said. "A noble little fellow, upon my word—and a Thetford from top to toe. Am I in season to be godfather!"

"Just in time; and we are going to call it Rupert; and I was just scolding dreadfully because you hadn't answered my letter, never dreaming that you were coming to answer in person! I would as soon have expected the man in the moon. And Aileen, too! And to think you should be married, after all! Oh, gracious me! Do sit down and tell me all about it!"

It was such a delightful evening, so like old times, and May in the possession of a baby, that Rupert and Aileen nearly went delirious with delight.

"And you are going to remain in England?" Sir Guy eagerly asked, when he had heard a resume of those past five years. "Going to reside at Jocyln Hall?"

"Yes; and be neighbors, if you will let us."

"Oh, I am so glad!"

"I promised Aileen; and now—now I am willing to be at home in England," and he looked fondly at his wife.

"It is just like a fairy-tale," said May.

"We haven't yet been to Jocyln Hall. We came at once here, to see this prodigy of babies—my wonderful little namesake."

Very late that night, when the reunited friends sought their chambers, May lifted her golden head off the pillow, and looked at her husband entering the room.

"It's so very odd, Guy," slowly and drowsily, "to think that, after all, a *Rupert Thetford* should be SIR NOEL'S HEIR."

Milton Keynes UK
Ingram Content Group UK Ltd.
UKHW011103080324
439029UK00005B/416

9 789357 953993